"So tell me, Cate," Noah asked. "Who's going to leave this time?"

"This time?" She tossed her head, letting the wind blow the bangs from her eyes. "Why, I am, of course," she said lightly. "As soon as the assignment is done."

"Of course you'll be the one to leave," he muttered, pulling her roughly against him. "But you're here now."

Excitement hit her with the power and the suddenness of a tidal wave. His body was hard against hers, his face taut with emotion, his eyes aflame with desire. She couldn't have moved if she'd wanted to—and she didn't. The moment was electric with possibilities, none of which were probably wise or sane. But she waited, her breath caught in her throat, the wanting inside her unbearable. . . .

One hand slid beneath her top and up her spine. His touch carried strength and certainty; his call-used fingertips brushed over her skin with possession. And then he brought his mouth down on hers in a kiss that extinguished thought. . . .

WHAT ARE *LOVESWEPT* ROMANCES?

They are stories of true romance and touching emotion. We believe those two very important ingredients are constants in our highly sensual and very believable stories in the LOVESWEPT line. Our goal is to give you, the reader, stories of consistently high quality that may sometimes make you laugh, sometimes make you cry, but are always fresh and creative and contain many delightful surprises within their pages.

Most romance fans read an enormous number of books. Those they truly love, they keep. Others may be traded with friends and soon forgotten. We hope that each LOVESWEPT romance will be a treasure—a "keeper." We will always try to publish

LOVE STORIES YOU'LL NEVER FORGET
BY AUTHORS YOU'LL ALWAYS REMEMBER

The Editors

STORM SONG

FAYRENE PRESTON

BANTAM BOOKS

NEW YORK · TORONTO · LONDON · SYDNEY · AUCKLAND

STORM SONG

A Bantam Book / February 1994

*If you would be interested in receiving protective vinyl covers for your
Loveswept books, please write to this address for information:*

Loveswept
Bantam Books
P.O. Box 985
Hicksville, NY 11802

ISBN 0-553-44415-8

Published simultaneously in the United States and Canada

PRINTED IN THE UNITED STATES OF AMERICA

OPM   0 9 8 7 6 5 4 3 2 1

To my "Swim Team"
for the beautiful music they bring to my life:

Bess Blackstone, Terry Cohen, Sally Epple,
Jim Garvin, Jeane Halford, Norma Kemmet,
Wistie McKee, Patrick Postell, and Gerry Ritts

PROLOGUE

"It's official," Susan Hilcher said excitedly. "McKane is going to be heading up a concert here at the Coliseum in two months and the entire proceeds will go to benefit AIDS research."

Noah McKane. Cate Gallin's hand tightened on her pencil, but she kept her focus squarely on her boss, who was so thrilled her voice was an octave higher than normal. Susan, the dynamic and exacting managing editor of the Los Angeles–based entertainment and news magazine *Spirit*, was as giddy as a teenager. Cate smiled. Susan was usually so cool, so poised and reserved. But even the thought of Noah McKane could do that to a woman, make her starry-eyed and foolish.

There was an excited squeal from the end of the table, and Cate looked at its source. Marcy Jenkins, one of the magazine's newest reporters. Cate didn't think she'd ever been as young as Marcy, even at the same age. She'd always been older than her years, overserious perhaps, and dedicated to becoming the best photojournalist she could be.

"Who'll be getting tickets?" Marcy asked, glancing around the table, a tinge of desperation in her voice. "I've *got* to go!"

Robert Moody, the entertainment editor, spoke up in his trademark world-weary drawl that nevertheless conveyed his intent. "*If* the magazine gets any tickets, they'll come to me, and if you think you're getting mine, you're crazy."

Marcy groaned.

Susan's frown was directed more to herself than the young woman. "Never mind tickets. The question is how can we get an *interview* with the man."

Matt, one of the magazine's veteran reporters, grinned. "Now, there's an idea for you, Marcy. All you have to do is get an interview with McKane, and chances are you'll get tickets."

"Yeah, right." Marcy slumped in her seat.

The price of a ticket would be exorbitant, Cate thought absently. Noah McKane had been news ever since he burst onto the rock and roll scene at the age of seventeen, a dark, brooding, and already formidable young man. His wasn't a fame born through hype, but rather of a phenomenal, compelling talent and gut-wrenching hard work. Now he was generally considered one of the greatest musicians and songwriters of his generation. And he had never granted an interview.

"I almost hesitate to ask this," Susan said, continuing with uncharacteristic sheepishness, "but does anyone have any *new* ideas about how we can snag him for a spread? Hell, I'd even do handsprings across the entire length of the Hollywood Hills for one little quote from him."

Matt, serious now, shook his head. "We've tried every trick in the book, as you very well know. But if *we* haven't succeeded, at least we have the consolation of knowing that no one else has either."

Marcy spoke up with a hopeful tone. "Okay, so he's never given interviews throughout his career, but maybe he'll do an interview in conjunction with the benefit. I mean, after all, he obviously cares about AIDS research."

Her naiveté brought laughter from half the people at the table. "Just lending his name to the charity brings all the publicity it needs," Matthew said.

Susan's brilliant red nails beat a nervous tattoo on the table. "I've tried everything I can think of to get to him, from bribes to key people I thought might be useful, to mutual friends. But nothing. *Nada*. Zip. It's almost as if he has something to hide, but then better newspeople than I have tried and found nothing."

Cate forced herself to relax her grip on the pen, but then several moments later discovered that she was holding it even tighter.

Gary Winthrop, Susan's superefficient assistant, grimaced. "Most people in the public eye will at least send out a polite refusal letter, but from his office all you get is a big fat nothing. I know, because every month I try a new approach. That man has a stone wall around him, and no one can get to him."

Cate looked down at the pen in her hand and heard herself saying, "I can get to him."

For a moment there was stunned silence, then everyone began talking at once.

The sound of the incredulous voices faded until she could no longer hear them. And she felt a sense of faint relief as a thought, barely formed, came to her.

I'll have a place to hide.

ONE

One Week Later

"Catherine Gallin," Cate said, automatically giving her full name which she used only professionally. Her identity had been queried by a male voice coming through a speaker imbedded in a stone column.

"Come on up," the voice said.

Iron gates swung open, offering entrance to Noah McKane's Southern California beach estate. She drove through, then glanced in the rearview mirror to see the gates closing behind her. Those gates would keep the world at bay. Those gates would keep all who resided inside them safe. She felt strangely comforted.

The driveway ahead curved gently, and as she rounded the first bend, the street noise already seemed distant. Farther along the upward slope through lushly landscaped grounds, she could hear only the chirping of birds, the faint clacking of palm fronds, and the distant whispering rush of the Pacific.

Emerging from a thicket of trees, she saw the house, an imposing stone structure that sprawled across the top of the hill against a backdrop of vivid blue sky. Clusters of red bougainvillea flanked the entrance, and white roses blanketed a trellis on the east wing of the house.

For months now she'd lived with a vague sense of tension, a tension that seemed to hover around her like cold air on a still winter's day. But as she viewed Noah McKane's house for the first time and realized that he was inside, waiting for her, the tension closed around her and layered itself over her skin.

As she climbed from the car, one of the carved teak front doors opened and a sleepy-eyed giant walked out. His spiked orange hair clashed violently with the brightly printed Hawaiian shirt he wore, and the scar that bisected one cheek added a sinister aspect to his face.

His expression was blank as he extended his hand. "I'm Cy."

"Catherine Gallin," she said as her hand was momentarily swallowed in his. He reached around her, opened the back door of her car, and leaned in to get her bags. "Maybe you should leave them," she said hurriedly. "I'm not sure I'll be staying."

"Might as well bring them in."

"Then leave the black bags. They contain my equipment, and I won't need them right away." She had achieved a point in her career where, if she wished, she could have an assistant assigned to help her, but she did so only occasionally. She didn't like anyone else handling her cameras. Besides, she preferred working alone.

"Might as well bring it all in now. Mac says you'll be staying at least one night."

She was torn between wanting to snatch her precious cameras from the grasp of the big man and reacting to the name he had spoken. "Mac? You mean Noah McKane?"

He straightened, bearing her varied assortment of bags. "Who else would I mean?"

Who indeed, she thought, pushing too-long wisps of honey-colored bangs from her eyes. Millions of his fans called him McKane, his albums listed the one name, McKane, but she knew from her research that there was a select group of people close to him who called him Mac.

Without a word she reached for the two bags that contained her two favorite cameras, sliding their straps off Cy's broad shoulders and onto hers. "Thank you," she said, wondering at the relationship between the big man and the musician. "Do you work for him?"

He looked at the bags on her shoulder, then at her. "I'm head of his security."

Because she did photo layouts of celebrities as well as of topical events, she'd had dealings with security, including the secret service on two occasions. In her experience, good security men were a breed apart; they saw everything and missed almost nothing. Cy appeared too big to move fast, too sleepy-eyed to see menace.

But then, in a twinkling, his drowsy eyes turned sharply alert, giving her the eerie impression he had read her mind.

"If someone tries to hurt Mac," he said, "they have to deal with me."

"I see."

"Do you?"

She was tempted to smile, except she wasn't sure she could remember how. "Your message is very clear, Cy. Your job is to protect your employer."

"You got it. Mac has never allowed a journalist within a city block of him for even a minute, but he's thinking about allowing you to move in for a few weeks. He hasn't said why he's doing this, and he doesn't have to. But *you* need to be aware that I recognize there are all kinds of harm."

How wonderful to be so protected, she thought wearily. How wonderful to command such fierce loyalty. What would it be like to feel completely safe and protected? Her imagination failed her: The concept was too foreign.

Having delivered his warning, Cy relaxed somewhat. "You could have knocked me over with a feather when Mac told me you were coming."

Her lips quirked. "Knocking you over with a feather is something that doesn't happen too often, I bet."

"*Never*. It never happens." When she didn't add anything, he motioned toward the front door. "Mac's waiting."

Cate fought to control her nerves as Cy led her through a series of wide halls and rooms. Colors around her dimmed, shapes blurred. She received the impression of space, luxury, and comfort, but she couldn't have actually said what the rooms looked like or how the house was decorated. It didn't matter. It was the owner of the house she was there to see, to capture on film. Seeing him would be the easy part; capturing him on film might prove impossible.

Cy finally led her into a big room at the back of the house. Despite the fact that it took a few moments for her eyes to adjust to the light pouring through the wall of glass that ran the entire length of room, she saw him immediately.

His tall, lean figure stood in dark relief against the light and the blue sky behind him. He was wearing a black shirt, open at the neck, and a pair of cream-colored slacks. His casually styled hair fell just past his collar in loose ebony waves. His presence radiated unqualified and absolute sexuality.

"Mac," Cy said, "this is Catherine Gallin, the photojournalist from—"

"Cate," he said, his dark eyes enigmatic.

His voice sounded like rough velvet might feel. Her fear and pain dissolved into warmth, but almost immediately formed again in the solitary depths of her soul, the place where the fear and the pain had resided for as long as she could remember. Something as simple as a voice could never change that, not even his, not anymore.

Outwardly her composure remained in place. "Hello, Noah."

He closed the distance between them and took her hand. "It's good to see you again."

Cy looked from one to the other. "You know each other?"

"We've known each other a long time. Haven't we, Cate?"

"A long time."

Cy's heavy-lidded gaze cut to her and stayed, but he spoke to Noah. "Would you like me to hang around?"

"Thanks, no. Cate and I have some things to talk about." His smile held an edge. "Don't we, Cate?"

"Yes."

"Okay, then, but call me if you need me."

"No problem."

"I'll put your bags in your room, Catherine."

She barely noticed when Cy left. From the moment she had entered the room, she had felt alone with Noah. Seeing him again, being close to him, made dizzying emotions swirl inside her. Warmth. Comfort. Heat that crawled through her. Levels of need, too many and complex to decipher. . . .

He slowly smiled, and this time his smile actually held a touch of humor. "You're looking well, Cate."

"You too." *Understatement.* He hadn't changed. He'd always possessed a dark intensity that compelled and commanded and, to a certain extent, controlled.

"And how long has it been this time?"

"Four years."

His nod was almost imperceptible. "Four years. You wouldn't stay."

"I couldn't." The room was quiet. Her voice was even quieter. But she could hear her heart pounding in her ears.

He slipped his hands into his pockets. "Yet you're here now. Why now?"

Her shrug was a reasonable facsimile of a nonchalant gesture. "These days, any time you perform it's news."

He stared at her for a moment, then turned and walked back to the spot where he'd been standing when she had entered. The glass wall wasn't solid as she had first thought. Sliding doors had been opened, allowing both the sunshine and the breeze inside. Noah stood in the doorway with his body half angled toward the distant sea that shimmered in shades of gray-blue.

She clasped her hands together and wasn't surprised to find them damp. Of course Noah affected her. He always had.

She crossed the room to him, taking her time, studying him, trying to discern what the differences might be between Noah in person and Noah of the paparazzi images she had seen in the last four years.

There were differences, *massive* differences, but nothing she hadn't known to expect. The simple truth of the matter was that he was so much more than a still, sometimes grainy image, and not for the first time she doubted her ability to capture anything near his essence.

Gentleness had not been used to mold his features. His face was made up of rough, abrupt lines, almost as if formed by erosion. His dark, onyx eyes could look like cold stone or hold shades of light, depending on his mood. His body was lean and hard, completely unyielding. He drew people and held them like some natural force. *She* was certainly drawn, always had been.

As she neared, his gaze came back to her, his expression sharp enough to shred the air between them. "I've often wondered why you didn't try to use your connection to me. Everyone else tries to get to me."

She wrapped her arms around herself. "I never felt as if I had the right to claim a connection."

His eyes narrowed. "If there is one person in the world who does have the right, Cate, it's you."

"I would never use you, Noah."

"And what do you call your asking to come here and do this shoot?"

"I won't be using you, Noah. It's important to me that you understand that."

"Then make me understand."

The hard glitter of challenge in his eyes caused her to shiver. "If there's anything you don't want shown, tell me and I won't shoot it. If there are certain times you don't want me around, certain places, tell me."

"Not want you around, Cate?"

His voice was husky, his tone slightly puzzled, as if he couldn't even conceive of not wanting her around, but she told herself not to read anything into it. The man was an expert with tones and words.

"The point is, I don't plan to barge in and rearrange your life, Noah. That's not the way I work."

"Tell me how you do work. I'm interested."

"I move in and stay until I feel I'm beginning to get to know the subject, the subject's situation, his or her people, his or her surroundings. Then I begin to take pictures, but as quietly and unobtrusively as possible. By that point, my subjects have usually forgotten I'm around."

His dark gaze swept over her. "I can't even imagine that."

"Noah, this doesn't have to be so hard." She had to force the words through a throat that felt as if it were moments away from closing completely. "I promise. I'm not here to harm or hurt you."

"But you wouldn't give me final photo approval."

"I couldn't. I can't. I'm sorry. I don't give anyone final approval on my pictures."

"And is that all I am? Anyone? Just another subject?"

"I hope you know better than that." Her voice shook, but there was nothing she could do about it.

She remembered her boss, Susan, practically jumping up and down, saying, "Are you *crazy*? Give McKane photo approval! Give him whatever damn thing he wants! Only get us the spread!" But Cate couldn't compromise—her photography was too important to her.

He regarded her broodingly, and her ever-present tension slipped below the surface of her skin. Even before his office had called to confirm, she'd known that he would allow her to come here to see him. She'd also known he would let her stay, at least overnight. But she was not at all certain he was going to let her do a photographic study of him.

It wouldn't matter if he didn't, she thought. Everyone at the magazine would understand. They were totally astounded that she had gotten this far. But as she well knew, getting this assignment went beyond what appeared on the surface. There was much more than what could be easily seen or readily explained—even to herself. The tension edged deeper through tissue and muscle.

"I know you've never done interviews," she said hastily, "but this won't be an interview. Just pictures."

"I've seen your photographs, Cate. They hit bone."

"I wouldn't do that, not to you."

"Why not? It would make you as a photographer. You'd be famous."

"I wouldn't do it," she repeated stubbornly.

"You might not set out to, but very few people know what you know about me."

His mistrust hurt. Hurt deeply . . . "Do you really think I'd use what I know against you?"

"The girl I once knew wouldn't. The problem is, I don't really know the woman, do I?"

"I wouldn't use it. I won't." She'd understood right from the beginning that it wouldn't be easy to see him again and talk him into doing the project. But she hadn't realized until that very moment how vitally important it was to her that he agree. "Let me stay."

His gaze glinted with something akin to danger. "I asked you to stay with me four years ago."

"That was different. If I'd stayed, we would have become . . ."

"Lovers?"

"Yes, but this is different. This is business."

"So what? What makes you think if I say yes we wouldn't become lovers this time?"

"We wouldn't. If it hasn't happened by now, I don't think—"

"There's always been a reason, Cate. Bad timing mostly. Have you considered that this time will be *the* time? Did you think at all about what might be between us when you thought of this assignment."

"No. I told you. I consider this strictly business."

"Liar. It's never been business between us."

"This time it will be."

Suddenly he reached out and wrapped his long fingers around her throat. For several seconds he stared at her, his thumb resting on the pulse point at the base of her neck. She fought to remain calm, to quiet her racing heart. She failed. His touch heated, excited, and made her despair. But then, without explanation, he dropped his hand.

Trembling, confused, she backed away, desperate to get a sense of reality back. Her gaze fell on a brilliant turquoise-colored glass sculpture. Placed to catch the light, it was shaped like an owl.

Her gaze continued around the room, taking in the lengths of chocolate-colored raw silk entwined with thick ropes of gold and rose and looped across the top of the glass wall and down the corners. Then she saw the richly colored Oriental carpets and the sofas and chairs done in neutral shades and piled with plump pillows. More brightly colored pieces of glass sculpture refracted the light. Original works of art hung on the walls.

She looked back at him, wariness in her eyes and reserve in the expression on her face. "You have a beautiful home, Noah. You've come a long way from the orphanage."

"I'd say we both have."

"Yes."

For a moment it was there, the bond that had existed between them since the moment they'd first seen each other at the orphanage—he a lone, solitary boy of ten, she only five at the time. And no one had been able to explain why the strange, aloof boy and the shy, golden-haired little girl had come together, least of all the two of them. But they had almost two years together in the orphanage before she was adopted, two years in which they grew to depend on each other. Self-consciousness had vanished between them. They had been able to lessen each other's pain and fears; they had shared and they had understood.

A line of concentration was drawn across his brow as he looked at her. "Is this assignment important to your career? I mean, are you depending on it in some way?"

Her head came up at his question. "I never depend on anything, Noah. It's better that way."

"You know what I mean." The deep growl of his voice demanded the truth from her.

"This assignment would be an enormous boon to my career, you know that. But my career will continue without this assignment. I'll still reach the top, it'll just take a little longer, that's all."

"Then why are you here?"

So it was all going to come down to the one question, the one answer. There were several reasons she could give him, and they would all be true. But there was one that was more true than the others.

"Because I need to be." There. She'd finally put what she'd been feeling into words, but she was incapable of explaining exactly what she meant, and she prayed he wouldn't ask her to.

With his dark gaze on her, the tension sliced deeper through muscles so tight, she felt actual physical pain. Her stomach roiled. She was going to be sick if he didn't say something soon.

"You can stay, Cate."

She didn't trust what she'd heard. "I can do the shoot?"

"You can start taking your pictures anytime you want. But if I become uncomfortable with the process, you'll stop. Agreed?"

She let out a long, pent-up breath. "Agreed. Thank you, Noah."

"No thanks are necessary. You wouldn't be staying if I didn't want you here."

By late afternoon, dark clouds were forming far out over the horizon. Cate had spent the past few hours unpacking and settling into the room, not a huge task, but one that she'd taken her time with. The grounds had beckoned her to explore, but she had resisted. She'd felt a real need to put her things in order around her, to hang and straighten the clothes she'd brought, to place her toiletries precisely, to check and recheck her equipment.

And when she'd done all that she could do, she lay down on the bed and tried to rest. But as had been the case the past few months, rest proved impossible. She couldn't remember the last time she had gotten a full night's sleep. Even naps had been eluding her.

And now, as she stared at the dark clouds simmering out over the horizon, she couldn't help but wonder if they held an ominous portent.

She exhaled shakily. What in the world was wrong with her? Her body did not possess a single fanciful bone, but unfortunately her imagination had been working overtime lately. Things had been happening that she couldn't explain. Shadows, sounds, telephone calls . . .

She picked up the phone and dialed her office.

Gary Winthrop answered. "Susan Hilcher's office."

"Hi, Gary. It's Catherine. Is Susan available?"

"*Catherine!* We've been waiting to hear from you. As a matter of fact, I expected you back by now."

"I won't be back for a while. I'll be staying at the McKane estate."

"You're *kidding!*"

"No. I got the assignment."

"Are you sure?"

Her lips moved, curving upward in a slight, appreciative smile. She couldn't blame him for his skepticism or even his suspicion. It must seem to everyone at the magazine that she had accomplished the equivalent of pulling a rabbit out of a hat. "Yeah, Gary, I'm positive."

He was silent for a moment, more than likely, she thought, trying to grasp what the spread on Noah would mean to the magazine. She had never thought too much about the business end of a magazine, only the creative. But there was no doubt that a spread on Noah was going to make sales of *Spirit* skyrocket.

"How long do you think you'll be there?"

"I don't know exactly."

"I'm asking because of the anniversary-issue shoot Susan assigned you. If you're going to take too long, we'll assign another photographer."

She pinched the bridge of her nose. She hadn't given any thought to the next assignment. Susan had given her the job only yesterday before she left the office, informing her she wanted behind-the-scenes pictures of what and who made the magazine run for the anniversary issue. "I'll be back in time for that."

"Are you sure? It's not that important. Anyone can do it."

"I'm sure."

"Well, congratulations, Catherine. Getting Mc-Kane to agree is a definite coup."

Yes, it was, she thought, for a myriad of tangled reasons. So when, she wondered, was she going to be able to relax and enjoy the fact that she had the assignment?

She heard a woman's voice in the background. "Is that Catherine? Give me that phone. *Catherine?*"

"Yes, Susan. I'm just checking in. Noah okayed the shoot."

"Noah?"

"McKane."

"You mean he accepted *no photo approval?* "

"Yes."

Susan let out a whoop of joy that made Cate jerk the phone away from her ear.

"Catherine, Catherine, are you there?"

Tentatively Cate returned the phone to her ear, ready to pull it away again at a moment's notice. "I'm here."

"Listen, this is the scoop of a lifetime, and we need to take full advantage of it. I want something spectacular. I want something stupendous. I want *dirt!*"

She sighed, having already anticipated Susan's reaction. "Susan, last week you didn't think you had a prayer of getting McKane. This week you've got him. Don't be greedy."

"But—"

"This spread is going to sell out all over the country, no matter how many we print and distribute. Besides, I don't *do* dirt."

"Honey, your photographs can expose the soul.

Give me that man's soul, and I'll give you your future on a platter."

Cate frowned. "Listen, I've got to go now. I'll check back with you from time to time. Bye."

"No, wait, I want to know—"

She hung up and stared blindly down at the phone. *Could she really hurt Noah with her photographs?* He had said something similar.

After a moment she shook her head, impatient with herself. No, if she thought for one second she might hurt him, she would leave. But she had no intention of hurting Noah. He was too important to her, always had been, even though as they had grown older they had seen each other less and less.

It didn't matter though. When she had been a child, he had been her world. She had grown up, of course, and her world had expanded, their relationship had changed, but he had remained very important to her. She supposed he always would.

TWO

A few hours later Cate paused in the doorway of the dining room. Noah was sitting at the head of the table, leaning back in his chair, relaxed, compelling, lazily smiling at something the woman next to him was saying. Cate had seen the woman before, staring out from hundreds of magazine ads, her extreme beauty effortlessly selling the product. She was supermodel Gloria Latham, tall, thin, soignée, and very, very beautiful. And Noah was smiling at her. . . .

Four other people were seated at the table, three members of Noah's band and another young woman. Cy was nowhere in sight.

The table was long and gleaming with woven blue and white mats at each place. The flames of innumerable short fat blue candles flickered among a thick garland of fresh flowers and edible fruit that ran the length of the table. The delicate tinkle of fine crystal mixed with the gentle ring of laughter. Everyone seemed very comfortable, like family, she thought. And she was to be the outsider.

Just then Noah's dark gaze locked on her, and he beckoned her in.

A horrifying moment of self-consciousness swept over her as silence fell and all eyes turned toward her. She was wearing a princess-style flowered cotton dress with buttons that ran from the scoop neckline to the calf-length hem. It was simple and inexpensive, like most of her clothes, easy to work in, easy on her budget. She'd never worried much about clothes, and under normal circumstances she wouldn't have cared that her wardrobe couldn't compete with the costly, casually elegant clothes the others were wearing. But with Noah present, a purely feminine instinct asserted itself, and she found herself hoping that she looked good at least.

Futilely she brushed a hand across her bangs to order them, then determinedly banished the self-consciousness. She was there to work, not compete with Gloria or anyone else.

Noah stood as she entered and motioned her to an empty chair at the near side of the table. When she was seated, he dropped back into his chair. "Everyone, this is Cate Gallin. She's going to be with us for a while."

"Hello," she said, her voice soft. No one returned her greeting, nor did they attempt to mask their hostility and suspicion. En masse, these friends of Noah's were daunting, but then, she sensed, individually they would be every bit as daunting. She didn't let it bother her. She'd already gotten over the biggest hurdle—Noah.

She glanced toward the head of the table and discovered he was watching her intently. A quiver of heated awareness ran through her and settled in the pit of her stomach. He'd asked if she'd considered what might occur between them when she'd decided to do this feature. Quite honestly, she didn't believe she had, but then she couldn't be entirely sure. Noah had never stayed exclusively on the surface of her consciousness. Oh, no. Long ago, he'd seeped into her blood, her heart, her bones, and she had no way of knowing how much internal damage he'd caused.

He smiled slightly as if he knew what she was feeling. "I should perform the introductions. Cate, on your right, next to you, is Chris Santini."

The band's rhythm guitarist, Cate mentally noted to herself, nodding to the good-looking man with the shoulder-length tan-colored hair and ice-blue eyes. Santini, as he was known, had quite a reputation with the ladies. Photographers rarely caught him with the same woman twice. Beyond his other obvious attributes, Cate decided, his eyes were his most intriguing feature. They would make a woman want to melt their iciness and see passion replace it.

"And next to Santini and between him and me is Gloria Latham."

Gloria acknowledged Cate with a barely perceptible incline of her head, but Cate thought she detected a hint of curiosity cross the woman's almost perfect features.

Noah continued. "Directly across from you is Dorsey Summers."

Dorsey was the band's bass guitarist; his hair was short enough to make a marine sergeant proud, and he wore round wire-rimmed glasses. He had a reputation for being dauntingly moody and very closed. He would have only so much patience for the human race, Cate thought, and then he would retreat.

"Next to Dorsey is Bonnie Stewart."

Bonnie gave her a lovely smile, and after the definitely cool reception she had been receiving, Cate nearly fell off her chair in surprise. Bonnie was a delicate, ethereal creature with long blond hair and china-blue eyes. She was wearing a dress in a creamy yellow color, and its filmy fabric did nothing to disguise the fact that she was pregnant.

"And finally," Noah said, winding up the introductions, "next to Bonnie is her husband and our drummer, Ian Stewart."

A tall, powerfully built man with shaggy hair the color of ginger snaps, Ian looked strong and big enough to bench-press a truck.

With the exception of Bonnie and herself, Cate thought, every person at the table was famous. She hadn't needed Noah to introduce them to her, but she appreciated his thoughtfulness.

She glanced around the table, her gaze stopping on each person in turn. "It's a pleasure to meet all of you. I'm sorry if I've held up dinner."

Silence.

She considered the group. From the very beginning, many years ago in the orphanage, she and Noah had tacitly forged an agreement to protect what was between them from others, so she was positive that neither the band nor the other two women present knew of the past she shared with Noah. And that was exactly as she wished it to be, she thought. She didn't want or need concessions from any of them. She created her own breaks.

And so she accepted the suspicion and hostility that hung thick in the air around her. She much preferred her foes to be out in the open, where they could be seen and faced.

"You didn't hold up dinner," Noah said, his quiet force stirring the thick air. "Did you have any trouble finding your way here?"

"Not too much." Earlier in the afternoon, when he had showed her to the guest bedroom, he had given her directions and the time for dinner. He had also told her to call him if she didn't feel she could find the dining room, but she was so used to doing things for herself and by herself that she had struck out on her own without even thinking.

Bonnie smiled at her once again. "The house is big, but once you get the general layout down, you won't have any trouble."

Cate returned the smile with gratitude. "That's good to hear. When is your baby due?"

Bonnie laid a hand on her rounded belly. "Three months, and we can't wait."

"Is this your first?" She didn't think it was general knowledge that Ian was married. She certainly hadn't known, so for all she knew they could have several children.

"The first, but hopefully not the last. And we already know our baby is a girl. We're going to name her Juliette."

"What a lovely name."

"Thank you. We think so."

Bonnie cast an adoring gaze at her husband, and Cate received her second surprise of the evening when the man whose face looked as if it had had a close encounter with a chain saw visibly melted beneath the gaze.

Across from her Dorsey shifted impatiently. "Exactly what do you think you're going to be doing here, Miss Gallin, and how are we all going to be involved?"

There it was, laid neatly out on the table for her, the question that no doubt everyone except Noah had been thinking and the source of the hostility and suspicion. A glance at Noah showed her he had no intention of interceding, which didn't surprise her. He may have known her longer, but in total time spent with him, the band would win hands down. Besides, it wasn't his assignment, it was *hers*.

She fixed Dorsey with a steady gaze. "Please call me Cate. I'd like it if all of you would. And as for what I'll be doing, Noah has given me permission to photograph him, and the spread will focus on him. But I'd also very much like to include you, Santini, and Ian. You're in rehearsals for the upcoming concert, and I also understand you're working on material for a possible new album. I'd like to try to portray the creative process a band goes through."

Santini snorted. "Good luck."

She turned toward him. "I realize that there's no way I can really show what you go through. It's too complicated, too internal. But I can show the external, the work that goes into this type of effort, the way you work together as individuals to make a whole, in this case a performance and a possible album." She paused. "That is, I can, if you give me your permission."

"I don't like anything about this," Dorsey said flatly. "We've never worked with a photographer around. Mac?"

"I think it will work out."

"But what if she does a hatchet job?"

"I won't," she said, speaking up before Noah could say anything else. "You have my word." She might have used her past relationship to gain entry to Noah's world, but now that she was there, she would succeed or fail on her own.

Ian made a rude sound. Dorsey exchanged a look with Ian and Santini, a look that only the men at the table could interpret. Finally he directed his gaze toward Noah. "I know we've already had a talk about this, but are you really sure, Mac?"

Noah slowly nodded. "I'm sure."

Cate watched as the three band members continued to look at him. Even though he had remained silent for most of the exchange, everyone in the room had been focused on him, including her. The men who comprised Noah's band were the crème de la crème of rock musicians. They could work with anyone they chose. They even had the prestige and talent to embark on solo careers if they desired. But there was no doubt that their loyalty was to the man who sat at the head of the table. And if it weren't for Noah, they wouldn't be giving her a minute of their time. They hated the whole idea, but with a flash of intuition she realized they hated the idea for Noah's sake, not theirs.

She cleared her throat. "Strictly speaking, it's not necessary for me to include the three of you— I can shoot around you—but including the three of you will definitely make for a better overall spread, plus it would make my job infinitely easier."

"We don't really care if your job is easy or hard, Miss Gallin," Dorsey said, each word a chip of ice.

Cate's lips quirked. "I realize that, Dorsey."

Gloria provided Cate's third surprise of the evening by speaking up. "When I heard Cate was coming here, I made it a point to mention her name to several photographers I know. And without exception they all spoke of her integrity."

Bonnie plucked two daisies from the garland that ran down the center of the table and stuck them into her blond hair. "Mac has obviously given this a great deal of thought and has decided it will work. Why not give it a try?"

Santini's cold blue eyes did not thaw, but nevertheless he was the first to give in. "Bonnie's right. Mac knows what he's doing. I'll cooperate."

Bonnie nudged Ian. He scowled. "Oh, all right."

Dorsey's expression carried a warning as he switched his attention back to Cate. "We'll be counting on that integrity of yours, Miss Gallin."

If she'd just run and won a marathon, Cate didn't think she could have felt any more victorious or tired. Her gaze instinctively went to Noah. Surrounded by his friends and the trappings of his wealth, he seemed invulnerable. But there had once been a time when it had been he and she against the world. Now she was alone against the world.

Ian slipped his arm protectively around his wife and sent Cate a hard look. "Bonnie is off limits when you have a camera in your hands, understand?"

"If that's what you want." She glanced down the table at the other woman. "Gloria, what about you? Would you rather I not photograph you?"

Hesitating, Gloria turned her head toward Dorsey, her expression momentarily revealing a hint of yearning. Then, professional model that she was, she quickly schooled her features.

But a light went off in Cate's head. *Of course*, she thought, perturbed at herself for not remembering sooner. Part of her memory must have been wiped out when she had walked in and seen Noah smiling at the beauty. According to the gossip column in *Spirit*, Gloria and Dorsey were a relatively new item. She mentally saluted the beauty. Gloria had to be a brave woman to take on the aloof, reserved musician.

Gloria finally gave a shrug of one enticingly bare shoulder. "Sure. Why not. If I'm around."

"Thank you," Cate said. "Look, everybody, I know how awful it is to feel that someone is constantly watching over your shoulder—"

"How do you know that?" Noah asked.

She blinked. Noah's quick question reminded her that he had once had the ability to see through her. She was going to have to be more careful, she realized. There were things Noah didn't need to know about her life. For instance, he didn't need to know that lately she had felt as if her life was unraveling strand by strand.

"You're right," she said, feeling exposed by Noah's sharp question and sharper look. "I don't actually know, but I can imagine what it feels like, and I promise to try to make this as painless as possible for all of you. I won't even start shooting for a couple of days, and by the time I do, I hope you'll be used to having me around."

"We'll see," Santini said while Dorsey and Ian frowned at her.

"It's definitely going to be interesting," Noah said, his expression closed. "Is everyone ready to eat?"

And as if he had given a signal, a door swung open

and a man and woman entered, bearing steaming dishes of food.

Cate glanced at the clock on the nightstand as she climbed into bed. Two A.M. She pulled up the covers and turned out the light, feeling incredibly weary. Maybe here, safely ensconced in Noah's compound, protected by high brick walls, iron gates, unlisted telephone numbers, and security, she'd finally be able to get a decent night's sleep.

But then again, she had never spent a night under Noah's roof, and it was doing crazy things to her nerves. During dinner she had learned that there were half a dozen bungalows on the estate. The three band members were staying in separate guest houses, as they always did when they rehearsed there. Ian was with Bonnie, Dorsey with Gloria, and Santini by himself. Cy and the security staff worked in shifts and lived in yet another house, and the couple who had served them dinner also had their own bungalow down the road. The rest of the staff came only during the day. That left Noah and her in the big house alone. Where did he sleep? she wondered. Was he close to her?

She turned over on her side, remembering the evening that had just passed. . . .

Dinner had seemed to stretch out endlessly.

Once the food was served, everyone but Bonnie and Noah set out to ignore her and she fell quiet.

After dinner Noah told her he and the band were going to be spending a few hours in the studio and asked if she would like to come along. She eagerly accepted the invitation.

Ian excused himself so that he could see Bonnie back to their bungalow. The rest of them walked with Noah across the moonlight-drenched grounds to the large state-of-the-art studio.

Once there, she took care to position herself in a big overstuffed couch placed well out of everyone's way, but it was obvious to her that the members of the band felt constrained in her presence, as to a certain extent did Noah. When after a couple of hours Gloria announced she was leaving to go to bed, Cate also decided to say good night. She'd achieved enough for today, she thought. Tomorrow she would try once more to make them comfortable with her.

Tomorrow she would get to see Noah again.

There had been a time she'd known exactly what he was thinking, but no more. He'd said he wanted her there, but he hadn't said why. He'd put his hands on her throat, on her skin, but he hadn't attempted to kiss her. Yet he'd brought up that time four years ago. . . . Four years ago . . .

❖━━━━━❖

Four years ago, Noah thought as he nodded his approval of a riff Santini had just blazed through. He motioned for him to keep working on it, took his own guitar, and dropped down in a nearby chair.

Four years ago he had nearly made Cate his.

After so many years of imagining that he saw her in the crowd at nearly every one of his concerts, one night he had finally looked out and seen her. During the drum solo he'd gone offstage and scribbled a note to her, then he had beckoned his road manager.

Back onstage, he'd watched as the road manager had made his way to her and delivered the note and the hotel room key Noah had told him to give her.

Even then he hadn't been sure she'd come. When he saw her leave before the encore, his heart had sunk. But when he reached his room, she'd been waiting for him.

Lying in bed, staring up at the ceiling, Cate still remembered the exhilaration she'd felt at being alone with Noah in his hotel room.

She'd attended several of his concerts over the years, but she'd usually been stuck with tickets up in the nosebleed section. This time, though, she'd saved her money like mad and paid the exorbitant price for a scalper's ticket in the third row. This time he had seen her. Looking back, she realized it was exactly what she'd hoped would happen.

When he arrived at his room and saw that she was there, he grabbed her to him and hugged her tightly. She almost cried with happiness. Having him hold her had felt so right, as if his arms were home to her.

He'd still been wearing the clothes he performed in, so he excused himself for a quick shower, then reemerged wearing a pair of jeans and nothing else. After instructing the hotel operator to hold all calls, he placed an order for room service, then sat down next to her on the couch and demanded to know everything that had gone on in her life since he had seen her last.

The excitement of being with him again quickly changed to an excitement of a different sort. His hair and skin were damp and emitted a sexy, fresh, masculine scent that made her want to bury her face in the fold where his neck met his shoulder and inhale. His chest was a blanket of dark, curling hair that made her want to burrow her fingers through it. A gold chain hung from his neck, and she remembered reaching out to touch it. . . .

❖———————❖

He'd been able to hold himself under control, Noah remembered. Barely. But when she reached out to touch him, he pulled her to him and kissed her as he'd been aching to do. His need for her had always been centered in his gut and in his heart. She was soft and sweetly pliable in his arms. And she tasted—Lord, it made him hard just thinking of how she felt and tasted that night. . . .

Room service had interrupted them, along with other "important" calls that were put through despite his instructions. It was her first real glimpse into the kind of life he led, and even though it was only a small window, she received the impression of a high-speed, high-powered life.

When the phone rang for yet the fourth time, he pushed her away from him in frustration, but he kept his hands on her upper arms in a tight, urgent grip.

"I have to leave tomorrow. We're flying to Europe. Come with me."

At first she couldn't comprehend what he was saying. The kiss rattled her senses, his nearness scrambled her thought processes. "You're leaving tomorrow?"

"The next twenty-four months of my life are

mapped out, and there's nothing I can do about it. Contracts. Airtight contracts. We're starting a world tour, and I want you with me." His eyes had glittered fierce and hot. "Dammit, Cate, we've been apart long enough!"

She'd been badly spooked. He had been asking her to give up her life. For that she needed some kind of reassurance, some kind of commitment. But she hadn't known how to ask for what she needed, and he apparently hadn't known how to give it. Or else he hadn't wanted to give it.

He pleaded with her, and she listened to every syllable, but not once had he mentioned the word *love*, not once had he asked her to come with him and spend the rest of her life with him. Rather, he'd asked her only to spend the rest of the tour with him.

And so she had walked out of his life, knowing she had to establish her own identity, personally and professionally, before she even could dare to think of joining him for a tour—or anything else.

Four years ago he'd desperately wanted her to stay with him, Noah thought, still caught up in the memory. He'd been cut to the quick when she said no. Since then, he made a valiant effort to leave her alone, as she wanted, and to go on with his life.

But more times than he cared to recall he found himself with the phone in his hand, about to dial her apartment. He knew the number by heart. And the knowledge that at any time he could reach her through the magazine worked on his mind, often nearly driving him mad.

And then out of the blue one day last week his office called him with her offer, and now she was there.

His first glance at her hit him in the gut, exactly where the sight of her had always hit him. And she looked just as he remembered. Tousled blond hair, as silky now as when she was a child. Clear green eyes that challenged, pleaded, and hid a myriad of mysteries. Long, strong, slender limbs he wanted wrapped around him. Lips he wanted to kiss until he was old and gray, or until eternity ran out, whichever came first.

There had never been a serious chance that he wouldn't let her stay. There were too many emotions still simmering between them.

This time he was determined. When she left again—*if* she left—they would have things resolved between them, one way or the other.

THREE

Cate awoke around eight o'clock, a time when she knew Noah and the others would still be asleep due to the late hours they tended to work every night. She had been there two days, getting to know the people around Noah . . . and wondering if she'd ever really get to know Noah again.

A look outside showed her that the storm clouds continued to linger far out at sea, but overhead the sun was shining. This aspect of her stay, this beautiful panoramic view of sea, sky, and landscaped grounds, was a gift, she reflected solemnly, a gift of peace she had badly needed.

She hadn't realized exactly how anxious and nervous she'd become during these past months until she started to feel herself begin to relax, a little at a time. Lord, she'd been wound *so* tight. Yesterday she had chanced a brief tour of the grounds.

Today, she decided, she would explore a little farther.

After a quick shower, she put on a pair of cream-colored textured cotton slacks and a matching loose top. Venturing downstairs, she discovered that with the exception of the staff there was no one about.

She had no idea how late Noah and the band had worked. Even though each night she had extended the length of her stay in the studio, she still left earlier than they did.

Santini, Ian, and especially Dorsey remained guarded when she was near. She didn't mind. She hoped they would soon realize she wasn't a threat to them, but rather a professional who wanted only to do a credible job. But if it never happened, so be it. As she well knew, nothing—life, work, relationships—was ever perfect.

And besides, it was Noah who held her attention, Noah who was everything, the sum total, the reason for her stay. And the only *turbulence* in this oasis of calm and beauty.

Taking a cup of coffee and a croissant from the kitchen, she walked outside. The sun warmed her skin, and the wind ruffled through her freshly shampooed hair, drying it.

Noah. There was an energy field around him that tended to pull in all who stepped into his domain. Resisting took a great deal of her effort. Being in his presence sapped her energy. Yet at the same time there was very much a sense that the awareness was mutual. More times than she could count she had found his dark, brooding gaze on her, and Lord help her, his was a gaze impossible to ignore. A powerful sensuality resided within him, smoldering dangerously, threatening to burn all who came near. And as much as she would wish it otherwise, a casual look from him, a brush of his hand, or even a softly spoken word could leave her shaken and needy, with every feminine instinct she possessed vibratingly alive.

She slipped out of her shoes, wandered down to the beach, and dropped onto the sand. Gulls called out overhead, and the waves broke, forming lacy patterns a few feet away from her.

Peace, she thought gratefully. In her life it was too rare. Unsure when a time like this would come again, she wanted to enjoy these moments. Sipping her coffee, she watched as a tanker moved slowly across the horizon.

Lost in thought, she started when Noah dropped down beside her, as primitive and compelling as the ocean beyond him, so vital and masculine, her breath was nearly stolen away.

"Good morning."

His deep, velvety voice scraped against her nerves. "Good morning." She took a quick sip of her coffee, willing its heat to relax her rapidly tightening throat. "I'm surprised you're up. You were still working when I went to bed; I thought you'd be sleeping late."

His gaze swept over her, stopping to touch on her shoulder, bared by the wide neckline of her top that had slid down. She tugged it up.

"I haven't been to bed yet."

Her fingers itched for a camera to capture his dark energy as it was now, set against the power and unpredictability of the ocean. With the sun reflecting off the water and onto his bronze skin, the light was perfect, highlighting the combination of toughness and sensuality in his features. "You worked all night?"

"Pretty much."

"In the studio?"

"No." He gestured with his thumb over his shoulder. "The room where Cy brought you when you first arrived—the den. It's off my bedroom and has a piano. I like to work there sometimes late at night."

She forgot about the camera for which she had just wished as she realized that his bedroom was relatively close to hers—down a long hall and through the big den. . . . "You worked alone?"

"I work alone a lot." His shrug was casual, but his focus on her was intent.

"I guess that surprises me," she said slowly.

"It shouldn't. Have you forgotten what I was like in the orphanage?"

How could she forget? He'd been a wild boy with a reputation for violence and danger who would let no one but her near. Only she'd been able to see beneath the hard surface to the vulnerability and hurt, and she hadn't been afraid of him. But now she found that she was a little afraid.

"You've changed, Noah."

"Not really. I'm still the loner I always was."

She shook her head. "But you're surrounded by people."

"Sometimes."

"Ian, Santini, Dorsey—"

"They're good friends, and we've been through a lot together, and we're very close, but—"

He frowned as if something displeased him, and she realized he was staring at the distant storm clouds.

After a moment he continued. "I've never been able to let them completely in."

"Why's that?"

He turned back to her, one dark brow raised. "Are you interviewing me, Cate?"

"No, Noah," she said, attempting to rein in her threatening sparks of anger. "I'm not an interviewer."

"Then what are you doing?"

"I'm—" She stopped, realizing she didn't really know. Since she'd arrived at the estate, this was as close as she'd gotten to having a normal conversation with him. During this short time with him, she'd forgotten her job, what lay beyond the estate's gates, the years that had separated them. The problem was, she couldn't really *afford* to forget, not anything.

"You're what?"

"Nothing. Shouldn't you go get some sleep?"

"I'm touched by your concern, but it's not necessary. Finish your sentence."

"I'm trying to understand. I remember how alone you once were."

His expression turned sardonic. "But I wasn't entirely alone, was I? I had you."

"Right," she said, determined not to let him rattle her. "And now you have all this." With a motion of her hand she indicated the house and grounds behind them. "If it's not enough to make you happy, what is?"

"What constitutes happiness for you, Cate?"

"I asked *you* the question."

"All of this helps—it would be stupid of me to say it doesn't—but it's not the answer. Now it's your turn. What makes you happy?"

"My career."

"And is it enough?"

"It's a great deal, Noah. Okay? It's a great deal."

"And who do you let close?"

No one, she thought. Absolutely no one. Her pain was intense, but quiet. Noah had been her first and only best friend—and then they had grown up, and she had lost even him.

He eyed her contemplatively, then reached out a hand to her and touched her cheek. "Don't be defensive, Cate. Not with me. Fundamentally I'm still the same person you've always known."

"I don't believe that, not for a minute."

The wind blew her hair into a flare of honey and gilt. He brushed his hand over her head, smoothing, gentling. "Believe it, because it's true."

She jerked away from him, unable to chance being gentled. As much as she'd enjoyed the peace earlier, she'd never expected it to last long. She'd always known she needed to keep her edge. This assignment and this stay on his estate was a respite, nothing more. "It's *not* the truth. When we were young, you could communicate only with me. Now you're the ultimate communicator. You reach millions with your music and lyrics."

His eyes mirrored the storm clouds far out at sea. "The same goes for you. Have you ever thought of that? Your photographs portray a thousand emotions that touch everyone who looks at them."

She stared at him with a new wariness, not understanding what point he was trying to make. "Well, then, how ironic," she murmured. "We were two people who could talk only to each other. Then we grew up and apart and chose careers where communication is key."

"Perhaps the ultimate irony is that now we can't talk to each other."

"We're talking."

"Sort of."

He was absolutely right, she thought. They were only *sort of* talking. There was a lot inside her he would never hear. She set her coffee cup aside and threw her half-eaten croissant far down the beach to a flock of gulls.

"Is that all you've had for breakfast?"

She couldn't account for the sudden anger in his voice. She drew her legs up and wrapped her arms around her knees. "I can always get something more if I get hungry later. Your staff is super efficient."

He reached out and encircled her upper arm with the fingers of one hand. "You're too thin."

She turned her head to look at him, irritated that after not seeing her for four years he had picked up on one of the things that had been bothering her in the last few months. "No, Noah, I'm not too thin." In truth, she *had* lost weight lately, but she could think of no reason why she should tell him.

Without warning his hand tightened convulsively on her arm, and now there was near pain in his deep velvet voice. "Hell, Cate, why haven't you come to me before now? You never even once asked me for so much as a lousy concert ticket. Why?"

"Lousy concert ticket, Noah? One ticket in the first ten rows can go for over a thousand dollars on the scalper market, surely you know that."

"*Why*, Cate?"

"You're hurting my arm," she said carefully.

He released her with an exclamation.

She rubbed her arm where he had held her. "Maybe I didn't want to be one of the many who ask you for favors."

"I have a system in place so that most people and the favors they ask never get to me. My office handles them. But I've given you my private phone number, and you've never once used it." Resentment etched his harsh features.

"I never needed anything." *Except him*, at times so badly she thought she would die and on so many levels she couldn't count.

"Apparently *not*." His words were clipped. "And when you wanted this assignment, you didn't use the number. You went through my office."

"It was business. I thought I should go through the proper channels."

"How very honorable. And dumb, Cate. Really dumb. You do realize, don't you, that you're lucky my office happened to mention your request to me? Normally they wouldn't. They just refuse all requests for interviews out of hand, because they know that's the way I want it. It was a total fluke that your request got through to me."

Her eyes widened as the force of what he'd said hit her. "That didn't even occur to me," she said, amazed at her own stupidity. She tried to laugh, but instead gave a half-sob of incredulity. "I guess I wasn't thinking straight. I was blinded by the need to . . ."

"To what?"

To get to you. She closed her eyes for a moment, dismayed at the words that had almost escaped her, but even more horrified she'd even thought them.

"To *what*, Cate?"

"To get the assignment."

As if she'd hit him, his head jerked backward. Several moments passed before he asked, "Do you ever wonder what happened? Why it never worked out between us?"

His question surprised her. "Timing. You said it yourself."

"It was more than that. A hell of a lot more than that. We might have had a chance if you hadn't been adopted by the Gallins. They took you out of my world."

"It wasn't only them," she said, instinctively defending the people who, even if they had never been able to understand her, had given her both love and a home. They were no longer alive, but they still deserved her loyalty. "What about your music? It took you places I couldn't come."

"I would have loved to have had you with me," he said harshly, absently massaging one hand with the other, "but I didn't want to take you to some of the places I had to go."

"I would have gone," she said perversely. "I would have followed you anywhere."

"I couldn't let you."

"Right," she said, bitterness coloring her words. "*You* couldn't let me. *You* made the decision without giving me a choice."

"You were too young," he said flatly.

I was old enough to love you. "I guess you're right." The sarcasm in her voice was directed at both of them. She took a deep breath and remembered. "Early on, I used to demand that Mom and Dad invite you to see us."

His laughter held ragged edges. "That was after you resigned yourself to the fact that they were never going to adopt me."

A small smile touched her lips. "I missed you so much when they took me away from the orphanage to live with them. I desperately wanted you to be my brother."

"It never would have worked. The Gallins knew that. Even then there was too much between you and me, and they didn't want me anywhere near their little girl. And every time I did come around, they acted as if they thought I would give you a communicable disease."

"They didn't know what to make of you, that's all, especially after they were told your history."

"Ah, yes, my history. Quite a history for a young boy, enough to scare everyone away. Except for you. God, you had courage."

New bitterness scored her short laugh. "Right, and then I grew up, and realized the senselessness of having courage."

"That's not true. I've seen your photographs."

She shook her head sadly. They were talking about two different things. "Mom and Dad thought you'd never amount to anything, and then you upped and proved their theory right by running away from the orphanage."

He looked down at his hand, clenching and unclenching it as if the memory carried violent emotions. "I had to get out on my own. I had things to do, to prove, and I couldn't do it there. But I tried to keep in touch with you."

With studied casualness she lifted a handful of sand and watched as it ran through her fingers, impossible to hold on to. She'd felt the same way about him when he'd come to tell her he had run away from the orphanage. He'd been fourteen and she'd been nine, and in that one moment she'd felt as if she'd never be able to hold on to him again, as if he'd never again be entirely hers. And she had been right. "I'll never forget being sixteen and getting my first kiss from you."

He made an odd sound. "You think *I* can forget it?"

"You must have kissed hundreds of girls by then. You were twenty-one."

"Not hundreds, Cate. And none of them was you."

Something about his expression made heat creep beneath her skin. "Yeah, well, I know it wasn't the greatest kiss you ever received, but I guess by that time you knew that I had developed a huge crush on you."

"A crush, Cate?"

She hesitated, wondering if she should retract her statement, but then decided that in this instance, the truth wouldn't hurt. "A crush. For several years I'd been romanticizing you like mad, and then you showed up at my Sweet Sixteen party, drew me outside away from the others to wish me Happy Birthday, and then—"

"I kissed you." He shook his head, his expression bleak. "I couldn't believe I'd done it. I sure as hell didn't mean to, but dear heaven, you looked so damned beautiful."

"Beautiful?" She gave a short laugh of disbelief. "Noah, I was all arms, legs, elbows, and braces. Oh, no, wait. I'd just gotten my braces off, hadn't I?"

"I didn't notice any braces when I kissed you,

but then, I didn't notice much of anything except how damned sweet you tasted." Unable to resist, he reached out and touched the softness of her lips.

From head to foot she heated, exactly as she had during that first kiss.

"But you were just a kid," he said roughly, "and I was having a hard time reconciling with the fact that you were growing into a woman. I mean, after all, you used to sneak down the hall and crawl into bed with me, and suddenly you were sixteen and had curves that I wanted badly to explore. And there were other things too. You were so innocent. I didn't want anything bad to touch you, especially me. I had to leave."

She made an exasperated sound. "Lord, you make me angry! I *never* considered you bad, Noah."

"You should have. You definitely should have. Besides, the next time I saw you, you were eighteen, about to start college, and my career had taken off. The Gallins wanted you to finish school, and they were right."

"Yet that time," she said, her nerves tingling at the memory, "it was more than a kiss."

He had contacted her and given her directions to a friend's house out in the country. She had driven there, excitement bubbling through her veins at the prospect of seeing him again. He was alone when she arrived. At first he had sat her down and demanded to know everything that was going on in her life. But soon they were kissing and touching and she would have done whatever he had asked. By then her crush had turned into love, or, at least, she reflected cynically, at the time she had thought what she felt was love.

In fact, here on this lonely windswept beach, with the one man in the world who had ever meant anything to her—even if there was nothing between them now—she could admit to herself that a deep and abiding desire for him had seeped into her eighteen-year-old bones that day and never left.

"You made me furious when you told me to leave. Lord, but you hurt me."

He lay his hand along her jawline in a soft caress. "I know I did, and I'm sorry."

His caress made her want to cry for everything unfulfilled in her, for everything that probably never could be. But tears were out of the question. She never cried. She abruptly stood, breaking physical contact with him. "Don't worry about it. I came through it beautifully. I put earplugs on whenever any of your music came on the radio or someone in the dorm played one of your tapes. My grades actually improved when your records went to number one and were played a lot, because I'd shut my door and force myself to get lost in my studies." She folded her arms and took several steps to the ocean's edge so that the cool water lapped over her feet. She'd been more successful at blocking out the music than she had been at blocking thoughts of him from her mind. "I also dated like mad."

Later she realized that subconsciously she was trying to find Noah in the boys she dated, but there hadn't been one of them who had been even a reasonable facsimile, and she hadn't been able to take any of them seriously. The dating, she remembered, had slacked off when it dawned on her that inadvertently she was letting Noah control her life. But the knowledge hadn't stopped her from wanting him.

He came up beside her. In an effort to banish the disturbing thoughts from her mind, she summoned a light laugh. "I got my revenge. I left you the next time we saw each other."

"I remember." With a light, barely-there touch, he turned her to face him. "So tell me, Cate, who's going to leave this time?"

"This time?" She tossed her head, letting the wind blow the bangs off her forehead. "Why, I am, of course. As soon as this assignment is finished."

"Of course, you'll be the one to leave," he muttered, pulling her roughly against him. "But you're here now."

Excitement hit her with the power and the suddenness of a tidal wave. His body was hard against hers, his face taut with emotion, his eyes aflame with desire. She couldn't have moved if she had wanted to, and, she decided, she most definitely didn't want to. The moment was electric with possibilities, none of which was wise or sane. But she waited, her breath caught in her throat, the wanting inside her unbearable. . . .

Noah's hand slid beneath her top and up her spine. His touch carried strength and certainty; his callused fingertips moved over her skin with electrifying possession. And then he brought his mouth down on hers in a kiss that extinguished thought.

Her eyes closed and a roaring came up in her ears. She was shattered. Since she'd matured, she spent her life either running to him or from him. And now she was caught, unable to go anywhere, held well and truly in his arms, and she couldn't deny she was exactly where she wanted to be.

He urged her to open her mouth wider; she did. He cajoled her into offering her tongue to him, she complied. He wanted to close his hand around her breast and feel her achingly tight nipple against his palm, and when he did she could only moan with pleasure. She had no restraint, no shame or defense. And she had no explanation.

Suddenly he put her gently away from him; she was completely disoriented. And ashamed. She struggled for breath, for reason, and for unblurred sight. His figure wavered in front of her as if he were being distorted by shimmers of heat. It was moments before she could see him clearly, standing as still as a statue, gazing out at the sea.

"There's a storm out there," he said huskily.

She wiped a hand across her eyes, trying to regain her composure. "It's been out there for the last couple of days. Storms are rare here. It'll probably dissipate before it comes ashore."

"Storms don't dissipate, Cate. They just grow bigger and bigger."

It was a warning she took to heart.

FOUR

Sound shattered Cate's troubled sleep, an awful, ear-splitting blare that came in rhythmic short bursts.

With a scream trapped in her throat, Cate sat straight up in bed, quite sure she was waking inside the nightmare she had been having. Cold sweat covered her skin, and her heart was beating painfully against her ribs. Disoriented, trembling, she rubbed her eyes and tried to focus. Images from her dream mixed with what she was seeing. Shadows lurked in the corners, threatening, intimidating. Shafts of light sliced through the darkness of the bedroom with the menace of an invader. Men yelled in the distance.

With a cry she clamped her hands over her ears, trying to block out the harsh, discordant, frightening noise. The door to her room burst open, and then Noah was there, dropping down beside her on the bed. She reached for him as if he were a lifeline and she were about to go down for the final time. Her hands grasped his broad shoulders and found warm skin layered over hard muscles.

With one quick, all-encompassing glance he took in the fear and tension that held her in its grip, then pulled her against him. "It's all right. Hang in here with me. It'll stop in a minute."

She buried her face against his chest, instinctively trying to shut it all out. "What is it?" she asked, her voice broken. "What's that noise, that light?"

"It's nothing," he said, caressing her hair soothingly. "It's just the alarm. Something's tripped it, that's all."

That's all. Her mind repeated the two words. He didn't sound upset or scared. He sounded as if everything was under control.

The sound stopped as suddenly as it had started, leaving a silence almost as loud as the shrill noise had been.

Afraid to test the quiet, Cate didn't move. She was safe in Noah's arms, and she couldn't be sure that she would stay safe if she left them. She'd been in his arms that morning, down by the water's edge. He'd kissed her with passion and spoke of a coming storm. Was this it?

The voices had quieted to a distant indistinct rumble. Noah's heart beat strongly beneath her ear; his masculine scent permeated her senses.

"Cate?" He straightened away from her but kept one hand on her arm, supporting her. "It's over, honey. I'm sorry that happened."

Bands of tension circled her chest and throat, cutting off her breath, threatening to suffocate her. She tried again to speak. "What was it?"

His expression revealing his concern for her, he smoothed strands of damp hair away from her face. "I told you, it was only the alarm. Someone probably tried to get onto the property. It happens occasionally."

His words did not comfort her. "*Someone*? W-who?"

The corners of his mouth turned up. "Some overly devoted fan."

"A fan?" she asked, her voice breaking on a sob that managed to convey both hope and relief. "You're sure?"

The sound of her sob cut straight to his heart. "Cate?" With a sudden muttered imprecation he leaned to the side and clicked on the bedside light. Straightening to look at her, he received a shock. Her eyes were huge and dark, her skin paler than he had ever seen it. She looked fragile, he thought, and very, very breakable.

His response was the same as it had been when he was ten and looked across the playground to see the five-year-old Cate standing by a broken and bent chain-link fence, alone and defenseless, one knee skinned. He had wanted to take care of her then, and he wanted to take care of her now.

His expression was harsh, but his touch stayed gentle as his long fingers smoothed over her face, wiping away the sweat. "Lord, Cate, I'm sorry. This is my fault. I should have told you about my security system. There's no way you could have been prepared for it. No one could who's not used to a security system on the level of mine. It's natural that it frightened you."

She listened more to the sound of his melodious voice than to his words. Quieting beneath his hands, she felt her tension ebbing and her heartbeat slowing to normal. "Do you know for sure it was a person? A fan?"

"No, but chances are—"

"*Mac? Mac?*" Cy came barreling down the hallway, shouting Noah's name. "Mac, where are you?"

Noah straightened away from Cate, putting a decorous distance between them. And as he did, he reached out and casually pulled up the thin strap of her shift. Dazed, her hand went to her shoulder. She hadn't even thought about what she was wearing or what she must look like. It was then that she realized Noah was wearing only a pair of slacks. His upper body was bare and showed bronze in the lamplight.

"*Mac?*"

His gaze on her, Noah called to Cy, "I'm in here in the guest bedroom."

Cy's head appeared in the doorway and his gaze went straight to Noah. "Are you okay?"

"We're fine."

Cy nodded and pressed a button on his walkie-talkie. "He's here. Tell everyone to stand down."

"Did you find anyone?" Noah asked.

"No, dammit, but the grounds and the house are secure, so there's nothing to worry about. He or she, whoever, is probably long gone and won't try again."

"She?" Cate asked, pulling the sheet up to just under her arms. "You think it could have been a woman?" A woman didn't sound right to Cate, although she wasn't certain *why* it didn't.

"Sure. At least half of Noah's fans are women."

Cy barely glanced at her as he was talking, his focus being Noah. Cate was left with the disturbing impression he was used to seeing Noah sitting on a bed with a half-dressed woman. "But you're sure it was a person? I mean it couldn't have been an animal, like a dog or something?" She'd felt so safe behind these walls. She'd much rather believe an animal had breached the security than a person.

"The security system is state of the art. It can tell the difference between a person and an animal."

"Thanks, Cy," Noah said, his tone polite but dismissive.

"Sure. Sorry you were disturbed."

"No problem." He waited until the big man left, then he took her hand. "Relax, Cate. It's all over."

She nodded. "Yeah, I'm sorry. I guess I over-reacted." An understatement if she'd ever heard it. And here she'd been congratulating herself that her nerves had been improving.

"Like I said, your reaction was understandable. You had no way of knowing what was going on."

She stared at him, trying hard to put this epi-sode into perspective. "You said this sort of thing happens occasionally? Why? Do people really want to harm you?"

"Not usually. Some are just out for fun, to see how far they can get. Others simply want to get closer to the person whose music has touched them, namely me. Some get it into their heads that my lyrics are talking straight to them. Usually the alarm system scares them off, and they never try again."

She folded her arms across her chest. "It would certainly scare me off."

"Unfortunately it doesn't scare everyone away."

She shivered. "I don't know how you can live like this."

"Everything's a tradeoff. The walls and alarms in exchange for being able to make the music I want."

"And does the security system work? Always?"

"It has up to now, but there's the nut element to consider. That's why I have Cy."

"Cy . . ." She drew in a deep, shaky breath, thankful that the nightmare had receded and that she was now awake. But she wasn't quite ready for Noah to leave yet. "He's obviously devoted to you."

"He was one of the first people I met after I left the orphanage. He found me sleeping in an alley and took me home with him." He grinned. "The place where he was staying wasn't too far above that alley in creature comforts, but at least it was a roof over my head. After a while he took off and did a stint in the military, but we stayed in touch. He's come in and out of my life ever since. When he's here, he handles security. When he's not, he makes sure there's someone who can."

She nodded and tried to brush her bangs off her face, but they fell back. She was really going to have to get them cut, she thought absently.

"Yeah, I could tell right away he was very dedicated."

His eyes narrowed at something in her tone. "He wasn't rude to you, was he? I'll speak to him immediately if he was."

"No, don't. I can take care of myself."

His expression softened. "You've grown into quite a woman, Cate. You're accomplished and strong—"

Her abrupt laugh interrupted him, and she saw his puzzled look. At that moment she felt more needy than she had ever felt in her life, but she didn't want him to know. Her pride wouldn't allow it. She made another brush at her bangs, more nerves than an attempt at grooming. "Sorry. I guess I'm just not used to compliments."

"Why not?" His expression darkened. "Why the hell isn't there a man in your life showering you with compliments? Or maybe there is?"

The atmosphere around them changed. Up to that point she had viewed him as a comforter, but with her fear pushed aside for the moment, her awareness of him as a man surfaced. She was alone with him on a bed in a pool of lamplight, and she felt hunger stir in her. "There's no one."

"And why is that?"

She gave him the easy answer. "I suppose the right person hasn't come along yet, and my profession keeps me pretty busy. You should understand that. You don't seem to have found the right person either."

He stared at her, his gaze so focused on her, she felt as if it could penetrate right through her skin. "Sometimes I wonder what would have happened if there hadn't been so many ifs in our lives."

"What do you mean?"

"There are a lot of ifs in our history. Haven't you ever thought about it? *If* I hadn't been afraid of tainting you with what had happened in my past. *If* you hadn't needed to finish school. *If* I hadn't needed to go out on the world tour. *If,* Cate. Don't you ever think of all the turning points in our lives that took us away from each other?"

"No." What was the point of admitting that she did? "Things generally happen for the best."

His expression hardened. "What is that? Some sort of clichéd philosophy you've worked out for your life?"

Some people would quail in the face of his fierceness, she reflected, but she had been exposed to his dark moods since she was five. No, it wasn't his moods she was afraid of, but rather his heated sexuality that continued to pull her to him time and again. And hurt her time and again. Calmer now, she lay back against the pillows and regarded him. "Clichés are common-place because over the years they've been proved right."

He slowly shook his head. "For most people, maybe. I don't buy it for us."

"Why? Do you think you and I are somehow exempt from the norm?"

His hand snaked out to the side of her neck. "I haven't noticed too many normal moments in my life, have you?"

She could feel the tension in him building. "Do you want me to feel sorry for you? I don't. You've got more than most men can even dream about having."

"But I don't have everything, Cate. Not by a long shot."

"No one does. No one."

"But you're here now." His voice suddenly had dropped to an ominous quiet.

She'd sensed it coming. "For a very short period of time and for professional reasons."

He leaned toward her, his eyes burning with dark fire. "Do you really think I let you stay here for professional reasons, Cate?"

He kissed her, his mouth on hers, fragmenting resistance before it could form with a passion so forceful it shocked her. His passion wrapped around her, blanketing her with its heat. Her hands flattened against his chest and discovered skin hot enough to burn. She relented, softened, and her arms slipped around his neck to bring him closer to her.

His tongue thrust deep into her mouth, giving her a sample of his taste, making her want as she'd never wanted before. But then, she'd always wanted him, she thought helplessly, in one way or another. Always loved him . . .

He lifted his head briefly, drew in a quick breath, then brought his mouth back down on hers. His hand went to her breast, his palm covering her, his long fingers caressing her through the cotton chemise. His touch was unbearably erotic, but her downfall was his very nearness. No man had ever overwhelmed her like this. She wanted to breathe him in, to soften her bones and flow into him until they were a part of each other. She wanted to have him come inside her and never leave her.

And the idea frightened her. She was no longer an adoring child who could climb into bed with him to comfort and be comforted. She was a woman with deep-seated needs.

She knew Noah too well and at the same time she didn't know him at all. Would giving herself to him be the solution, or would it compound the problem?

She didn't know the answer, and she didn't feel up to figuring it out. She pressed her hands against him and pushed away.

"What are you doing?" he asked harshly.

"Trying to survive."

"We survived *together* when we were kids."

He looked so angry, she reflected, it might be impossible to soothe him even if she wanted to. "We haven't been kids for a long time."

"Right, and all our adult lives we've just missed connecting with each other, but maybe this is the time, *our* time."

"No." She shook her head, refusing out of hand to believe what he was saying.

"What's wrong, Cate? What are you afraid of?"

What was she afraid of? she repeated to herself, lying back against the pillows and closing her eyes. The answer was nothing. And everything.

Phantoms.

Ghosts.

Heartache.

Lately she had felt that she was holding on to the control of her life with the tips of her fingernails. And she was scared to death to find out what would happen if she let go.

Sleep didn't return easily to Cate. She lay in bed, her body aching, her lips tingling, her eyes wide open, recalling Noah's last words.

She was still awake an hour later when she heard the thunder. She slipped from the bed and opened the drapes. The outdoor lighting that surrounded the house allowed her to see that a finely textured rain misted the window and that the wind had picked up, blowing the palm fronds so that they clacked furiously. Occasional flashes of lightning illuminated the sky, and periodic claps of thunder punctuated the silence.

She drew the drapes and returned to bed, but still could not rest. She knew the rain would soon blow past, and the thunder would die out. It wasn't a true storm, only a bit of turbulence that would soon wear itself out.

But there was an instinct in her she'd never been able to deny. When she heard thunder, when she saw lightning, she wanted to reach out to Noah. And tonight that instinct wouldn't die.

She picked up the phone and punched out the three numbers Noah had told her would reach his bedroom on the house's interior phone system.

And all the while she told herself that she was being stupid. For all she knew, he could have gone out to the studio to work. Or he could even be asleep. Whatever, she was probably disturbing him. She started to hang up.

"Yeah, what?"

"Noah?"

"Cate?"

His voice sounded strained and distracted, as if she had caught him in the middle of something.

"Are you all right?" he asked.

"Yes, yes, I'm fine. Did I interrupt you? Are you working?"

After a long moment of silence he said, "I decided not to do any more work tonight."

"Oh." She felt foolish, because she had no real reason for calling him. She glanced over at the drapes and saw the fabric brighten with the lightning behind it. A loud clap of thunder followed, indicating that the storm was very close now.

"Cate? Was there something specific that you wanted?"

The strain in his voice was increasing. She shouldn't have called him.

"No, not really. I guess I just wanted to thank you for coming to check on me earlier. The alarm did scare me."

"I know. Are you sure you're all right now?"

"Yes, I'm fine."

"Good, then listen, I'll see you tomorrow."

"Right. Well, good night."

"Good night."

She hung up the phone, calling herself twenty kinds of stupid. What must he think of her?

Not too far away, in his dimly lit bedroom, Noah stared at the phone. His hand was clenched so tightly around the receiver, the tendons ridged the back of his hand and the veins showed prominently.

Overhead, thunder crashed. He flinched, but he didn't let go of the receiver. Outside the tall, undraped window, lightning streaked across the sky, briefly illuminating the faint line of sweat across his top lip and the muscles in his forearm that were roped with the desperation of his grip.

As if it were some sort of lifeline, he hung on to the phone until the last of the storm faded away.

FIVE

Cate focused her camera on the sparkling blue water of the swimming pool. From her seat at an umbrella-shaded table, the pool looked clean and inviting, but she had no intention of going in. It hadn't occurred to her to pack a swimsuit; she couldn't even remember the last time she'd worn one. She'd just come from an assignment to Africa and a famine-stricken desert. The assignment before that one, she'd been in a formerly communist country, chronicling the struggling stages of an infant democracy. There hadn't been a swimming pool in sight in either place.

She tightened the focus on Dorsey, floating on a raft in the middle of the pool. He was wearing mirrored sunglasses, making it impossible for her to tell whether he was awake or asleep, being enigmatic even in relaxation. Without thinking about it, she clicked off a series of shots.

"Have you started taking pictures, Cate?"

She lowered the camera and smiled at Bonnie, who was looking exquisitely feminine in a maternity swimsuit beneath a Grecian-style silk coverup that dropped from one shoulder to her rose-colored toenails. "I'm not getting too serious about it yet. It's simply that I can manage only so long without a camera in my hands before I go into withdrawal."

With a nod of understanding, Bonnie sat down in the padded chair beside Cate. "Ian's that way with his drums, and the guys are that way with their guitars. I plan to be that way with my baby." She rested her hand on her stomach with a contented sigh. "No nanny for this child."

"Lucky child," Cate said.

Bonnie cast a loving glance over her shoulder at her husband, who was lying on a double-width lounge chair, keeping a protective eye on her. "Yes, Ian is going to make a wonderful father, isn't he?"

Cate smiled wryly, positive no one in the world saw Ian in quite the same way as Bonnie did. She murmured something noncommittal just as Gloria sauntered out of the pool house in a shorts and top outfit that, Cate reflected, had probably cost more than she paid in a year for groceries. Apparently incapable of making an ungraceful move, Gloria walked around the pool. When Dorsey didn't stir, she strolled over to Santini, who was lying on another chaise and dropped down beside him. As she did, she said something that made him laugh.

Bonnie groaned. "Lord, she makes me feel like a hippopotamus."

Cate laughed. "Trust me, you're anything but. Plus, you're so radiant, I feel totally lackluster beside you."

Bonnie eyed her thoughtfully. "Do you plan to have children?"

The question temporarily stumped Cate. "I think I'd love to be a mother, but somehow I don't see children in my future."

"That's too bad." She paused as she adjusted her weight in the chair, then returned her hands to her oversize belly. "Are you beginning to feel at home here?"

"Feel at home?" She searched for a tactful reply and found it. "Noah's home is extremely comfortable."

"That's not what I mean. You seem so, I don't know, I guess *tense* is the best word."

And here she'd thought that Bonnie was wrapped up in her impending motherhood. Her lips twisted into a wry grin. "You're probably mistaking concentration for tension, that's all."

"Concentration? On what?"

"I'm trying to take everything in so that I can do the best job possible."

"We're really not that hard to figure out, Cate. We're just regular people, that's all."

Cate had to smile. "Regular people to *whom*, Bonnie?"

"To us. To people who really know us." She reached over and patted her hand. "Relax, Cate. It'll all work out. You'll see."

"I'm sure you're right," she said as much to placate Bonnie as to placate herself. After a lovely smile that beamed approval in Cate's direction, Bonnie rose and strolled back to her husband. He straightened and reached out a hand to help her down to the low chaise.

On his float, Dorsey slid his glasses atop his head. With a murmured word to Santini, Gloria stood, took several steps, and dove cleanly into the pool to surface beside him with a bright laugh and a big splash. He gave a war cry, slid off the float, and gave chase.

Mentally cringing at the idea of what the chlorine would do to the shorts outfit, Cate raised her camera. An unguarded Dorsey at play with a woman who commanded thousands of dollars for a few hours posing was too good to pass up. She caught the aloof guitarist and the elegant beauty frolicking, water droplets frozen in the air around them like crystal beads shot through with sun.

"Hey, Mac," Santini called. "About time you showed up. You going in?"

"Not now."

Cate jerked her camera away from her face as Noah strolled toward her, and she sucked in a breath at the sight of him. Sex and assurance oozed from him as he sauntered past banks of flowers with the lazy power and confidence of a man who was born knowing how to command the attention of tens of thousands of people with the slightest gesture. He wore tight black jeans and an indigo-colored shirt, its sleeves rolled up his forearms.

Her mouth went dry. He was yards away, but the air around her felt as if it was sizzling. She needed sunscreen, sunglasses, maybe even a concrete bunker, *something* to shield her from his effect.

She was barely able to stop herself from groaning aloud. The way she reacted to him was pitiful. Somehow she was going to have to rediscover her objectivity if she was to do a credible job on this shoot. Then again, she reflected ruefully, that just might be an impossible demand on herself considering she had never had any objectivity about Noah.

He dropped into the chair that Bonnie had occupied, his presence creating an electrical charge so strong, it almost assaulted her. He nodded toward the camera. "You've started your assignment?"

She carefully set the camera on the table. "I started my assignment the minute you told me I could stay."

He shook his head, smiled enigmatically, and let his gaze stray to Ian, who was adjusting an umbrella over Bonnie. "Why did you call me last night?"

His question caught her off guard. "I—I told you. I wanted to thank you for coming to check on me. If you hadn't, I don't know . . ." Her words trailed off as she remembered the fear she had felt at being awakened by the strident blare of the alarm.

He looked at her. "You don't know *what*, Cate?"

"I'm sorry about calling you. I had a feeling I was disturbing you in the middle of something."

He sat back, his face set into hard, unreadable lines. "Did you?"

"Hey, Mac," Gloria called. "Come in and help me get Dorsey!"

He turned in his chair just in time to see Gloria put two hands on top of Dorsey's head and push him under the water. "It looks to me as if you're doing fine on your own." He straightened, a formidable frown creasing his forehead. "You're never going to get to be friends with them if you persist in staying to yourself like you do. Why aren't you in the pool?"

His circuitous train of thought made it difficult to know what was on his mind. "I'm not here for a holiday, Noah, and I'm certainly not here to make friends. Besides, I doubt if it would be possible to be friends with them. They remind me of the Greek gods who used the world as a playground and only played with each other."

"And if they remind you of gods, what do I remind you of?"

"Zeus."

He shook his head, his eyes dark with disappointment. "I thought you of all people knew better than that."

His disappointment in her evoked pain and left her shaken, but not wanting to betray herself, she rushed on. "Besides, none of them trusts me, not even Bonnie, although she tries to make me feel welcome."

He looked at her for a moment, blatant calculation in his gaze. "When it comes right down to it, I don't trust you either."

More pain. "I know you don't, but, Noah, I told you I wouldn't do anything to hurt you with this photo spread, and I meant it."

"Photo spread, hell. *Forget* the damned assignment."

"If you're not talking about the assignment, then what in the world *are* you talking about?"

"My heart, Cate. You've trampled on it too many times—*that's* what I'm talking about."

Her whole body jerked in shock. "Excuse me? *I* trampled on *your* heart?"

"You don't think you have?"

"Noah, you're the one who has always—"

He muttered a harsh epithet. "We just can't seem to get beyond it, can we?"

"Beyond what?" She was totally bewildered.

"Let's get the hell out of here and go somewhere where we can talk." He grabbed her hand and pulled her to her feet.

"Wait," she cried, startled. "My *camera*."

"Leave it," he said tersely, striding away, dragging her after him. "It'll be fine."

"Hey, Mac," Dorsey called from the pool, concern in his voice. "Where you going?"

Without looking back, Noah raised his free hand. "We're going for a walk. We'll see you all later."

"Oh, great," Cate muttered. "Now they're really going to wonder about me."

"If you'd made an effort to get to know them, they wouldn't have so much to wonder about."

Her mouth dropped open. "Make an effort to get to know them? Noah, I—"

"Never mind," he snapped, lengthening his stride. "We're going to talk; now, where do you want to do it? The house? The studio? The beach?"

Cy suddenly appeared out of nowhere, standing in their path, his big body tensed. He looked, Cate thought half hysterically, ready to take her off Noah's hands if she was causing too much trouble. A brusque gesture from Noah made the big man move aside, and they passed by him.

"I don't suppose it would ever cross his mind that *I* might be the one who needed saving," she grumbled.

"He knows better than to interfere."

"Interfere with *what*?" She abruptly yanked her hand free and came to a stop on the slope of the thick green lawn. Unfortunately she knew the people around the pool could still see them and were watching them curiously.

Noah came to a halt and looked back at her with a harsh frown. "Why'd you stop?"

"Okay, Noah, now pay attention. I know this will be a hard concept to grasp, but give it your best shot. *I* am the one who doesn't have to do what you want. Got that? And the fact of the matter is, I don't want to go *anywhere*. Are you with me so far? I was perfectly happy where I was."

His unyielding expression showed he wasn't moved by her show of independence. "Tough, real tough. You're just going to have to adapt to another place. The only question is where. Do you want to go back to the house? Or how about the studio? It's soundproof."

"Why aren't you listening to me?" Her voice rose on each word. "And while I'm asking questions, why would we need a place that's soundproof? What do you have planned? *Torture?*"

He eyed her levelly. "Where's it to be, Cate? Make a decision, or I will."

Her teeth ground together. "I might be able to make a decision if you'd tell me why we're doing this."

"Because we need to talk."

"You keep saying that, but I still don't know about what."

"You know, but you won't admit it to yourself." He let out a long, heavy breath. "Okay, okay, it's everything that's happened between us from the time you were sixteen. It's there between us, and we can't seem to get past it."

At the moment she couldn't think of anything that sounded more like pain to her. "Why on earth do we have to rehash the past?"

"To see what's on the other side. Aren't you even curious?"

"No. Not one bit."

"You're either lying or you're a coward."

"I'm neither." But even as she said it she knew she was both—lying and a coward.

"The house," he said decisively.

She bit back an angry retort. "The beach," she said quickly. The outdoors would definitely be safer. She didn't think that even his vast house could contain his storm-filled emotions just then. He reached for her hand, but she pulled away. "I can get there under my own power."

Neither of them spoke as they walked. At some point before they reached the sand, Cate stopped and took off her shoes.

Noah paused to watch her. She was wearing a pair of oversize shorts and a top made out of peach-colored cotton, its rough texture emphasizing the smoothness of her skin. Anger had flushed her cheeks and darkened her eyes to a forest green. She appeared so rigid, she looked as if a good strong wind could snap her in two. And she was frustrating the hell out of him. He hadn't been able to concentrate on his work since she'd arrived, but that was about to stop. With a silent oath he stripped off his shoes as well.

A short time later they reached the beach that stretched as far as she could see in both directions; it was pristine and deserted except for the two of them.

Cate could feel his agitation. Unaccountably exhausted, she dropped to the sand. When he did the same, she made the decision to go on the offensive. She couldn't imagine what he hoped to accomplish by this confrontation, but the sooner it was over, the better for her.

"Okay, Noah, what is it? Do you want me to say I'm sorry that four years ago I didn't go on your tour with you? I'm not. Okay? I'm not! At that point in my life you would have become my entire world, and that would have been a catastrophe."

"Not for me," he said flatly.

A laugh escaped her. "Yes, Noah, eventually it would have been. Night after night you played to stadiums full of adoring people. You didn't need to come back to the hotel and find me there, doing nothing but waiting to adore you too."

"How the hell did you know what I needed?"

"I guess I didn't, but I knew that *I* needed something then that you couldn't give me." An unexpected flash of intuition gave her pause—no matter what she said, she would have gone anywhere if he'd only given her some sort of commitment. But he hadn't.

"How do you know I couldn't give it to you? You didn't ask."

"I didn't think I needed to."

He looked at her for a moment, then slowly nodded. "Okay, maybe you're right. Maybe I screwed up."

"I didn't say that. It was just the wrong time, for both of us."

"There's that word again. *Time.*"

If there was a point to dredging up the past, she was completely missing it so far. "Okay, but so what? We both made it through, didn't we? I mean, it's not as if either of us was broken beyond repair by any of those past what ifs."

"Beyond repair? No. But how about cracked and cracked pretty damned bad."

"*You*, Noah? You were hurt? *I* hurt you?"

Now it was his turn to laugh, a short bark of a laugh. "What's the matter, Cate? Have you forgotten how I can hurt?"

"I remember all too well how you used to hurt when we were young and had only each other. We grew up and things changed. You're talking about two different times in our lives, two different circumstances."

"What I'm talking about is the fact that I can feel pain. Still. And that you, Cate, can hurt me more *easily*, more *deeply*, and more *permanently* than anyone on the face of the earth."

She drew in a deep, stunned breath.

He nodded, his expression grim. "It's true. It's absolutely true. And quite frankly, I'm amazed you didn't know it."

She made a vague gesture. "But so many years have passed . . ."

He reached out and grasped her upper arms, his long, elegant fingers making bracelets around her skin. "So you're telling me that I don't affect you in the same way anymore? That I don't have the power to hurt you or wound your soul?"

She swallowed against a constricted throat. "That's giving you an awful lot of power over me."

"You've got even more over me. You can flat out cripple me, sweetheart."

She could feel herself beginning to tremble and brought her arms up to release his grip so that he couldn't. "Noah, this doesn't make sense. We haven't seen each other in four years! Not *once* have you tried to see me."

"How do you know? How do you know how many times I've picked up the phone to call you?" He moved his hand abruptly. "Never mind. Just answer this: Why did you call me last night?"

"I told you," she said. "I wanted to thank you for coming to check on me when the alarm went off."

"No, Cate. Give me the *real* reason."

"How do you know that isn't the real reason?"

"I don't," he said quietly. "I'm only hoping."

She caught a fleeting glimpse of vulnerability in his eyes, and as brief as the glimpse was, it was enough to make her capitulate. "The storm. It was the storm. I wanted to make sure that you were all right. Silly of me, wasn't it?"

She'd given him what he wanted, she thought. She hadn't been able to help herself. No matter how much she might deny it, he could still get to her as no one else. Tentatively she reached out to him, her voice and touch soft. "I still care about you, Noah. You must know that. Nothing will ever change my feelings." He turned to her, his eyes narrowed and burning with some inner emotion that made her swallow hard. "But you're talking about a different kind of caring, aren't you?"

"That's right."

"I can't."

"You can't what? Talk about it or give me a different kind of caring?"

"Both."

"That's bull, Cate."

"What is it you want from me?" she cried. "I don't *understand*."

"Then you're not paying attention. I told you. I want us to put the past behind us. I want you to understand once and for all that when I walked away from you on your sixteenth birthday, it was because I was already a man, and you were a girl, an innocent girl, and I knew if I stayed, you wouldn't be an innocent girl for long. When you were eighteen and I walked away, it was because you needed to finish school and I had a career that was taking off faster than I could handle. But know this—I wanted you even then."

She could take a lot of things with equanimity, but hearing him acknowledge that he wanted her wasn't one of them. "I don't see the point in this, Noah."

"That's because you don't want to."

"We should drop this, we really should."

"Not a chance. Four years ago there were no more reasons why we couldn't be together. And I wanted you with me so badly, I thought I'd die of it, but that time you were the one who walked."

When she opened her mouth to protest, he held up a hand, stopping her. "Okay, it was only fair. I had gotten my career established and you needed to do the same. I was hurt, you were hurt. We've both been hurt. But this is the *present*. Can we agree to be over the hurt now, in the present?"

She stared at him, flabbergasted. "That's really rather amazing the way you just managed to neatly summarize our relationship."

"Yeah," he said grimly. "Too bad it wasn't that easy to live through those years."

His remark stung. "Once your career got going, it didn't appear too hard for you."

"I had my music, but I didn't have you, now, did I?"

She couldn't seem to stop herself from asking. "And you wanted me?"

"Oh, yeah." His tone was definite and flat. "I wanted you."

They were getting nowhere, and she didn't know how much longer she could continue to fight him and to maintain calm, at least on the surface. "Okay, Noah, it's behind us. Is that what you want to hear? I agree with you. Hanging on to the past is pointless. So now what?"

"So now we go forward . . . or we don't. But we have to decide."

"Forward?" she said faintly.

"*Together.*" His expression was grave and resolute. "We go forward together. Or we don't."

"Noah, I'll always be your friend—"

"I hope so, but if I have my way, you'll be a hell of a lot more than my friend."

"You make it sound so easy."

"Nothing you and I have ever done, either together or apart, has ever been easy." His voice lowered and its velvet texture roughened. "But this just might be if we let it. Let's forget the past, Cate, and go forward from here."

She couldn't speak. For years there'd been nothing but obstacles between the two of them, those put there by other people and those put there by themselves. She was used to barriers. But now he was saying there were none.

"This doesn't make sense. What's changed? What's different this week from last? Noah, I was an *hour* away from you last week and all the other weeks before that one, living and working."

"You're here now."

"So that's what's changed? The fact that I asked for the assignment and came here? Noah, what if I hadn't asked?"

"I guess that's another one of those what-ifs that we'll really never know. But I wouldn't bet against me having gone to you sooner or later. You would lose if you did."

"You would have come to me? Really?" Hope layered her voice.

"Definitely. But you came here and you've stayed. Don't you see? Since you were adopted and left the orphanage, we haven't spent more than a few hours together at a time. We haven't had a chance up until now. I think we were always meant to be together, but our problem has been finding the right time."

She propped an elbow on top of a drawn-up knee, then dropped her head into her hand. "You're going too fast."

"No, Cate. It's more like I've gone too slowly up until now."

"I feel like the world as I have known it has been turned upside down. This is a lot to take in. I know you're used to people falling in line with what you want, but—"

"You're the exception in my life. You always have been." He circled long fingers around her wrist and tugged until she lifted her head and looked at him. "What's bothering you, Cate?" His voice was very gentle now, deliberately caressing her agitated nerves. "Does trying to start fresh with me scare you so much?"

She thought about his question and decided, *yes*. Simply put, she was terrified. All she'd ever wanted was to be with him, and now he was handing her dream to her, saying in effect that there was a possibility that all she'd ever wanted could be hers. It was too much. Like someone starved suddenly presented with a banquet, she felt overwhelmed.

She was no longer young and naive. She knew how hard the world could be, but she'd made it on her own with sheer tenaciousness and grit. She'd worked to banish vulnerability from her life, but now without the barriers between them she felt strangely vulnerable.

"Yeah, I admit it, it scares me. But understand it's more than that. Because of the past, because there's always been something standing in the way, you and I really have no idea how we feel about each other. Not really. We're old friends who've never had a chance to learn to be anything else, no matter what we might have wanted at different times in our lives."

He nodded slowly. "Maybe and maybe not. I think we've always been more than friends. The day you came here, you told me you needed to be here. I didn't ask you why then, but I am now. Why?"

She shook her head, experiencing the same helpless feelings she always did whenever she tried to sort out exactly what was wrong in her life. "It's complicated. There's the career opportunity of this shoot—"

"You told me you'd make it without this assignment, and I believe you. You're already halfway there. There's got to be something more."

She shrugged uneasily. "I wanted to see you again. Is that a crime?"

"You could have seen me anytime. You have my unlisted phone number, for God's sake."

"And you could have called me at the magazine."

"I know I could have, and I wish to God I had, but we're talking about now."

She sighed. He was right. There was something more. But how could she tell him about her fears? She wasn't five years old anymore, looking to him to make her world right with an understanding smile or a warm hug. No, making her world right was *her* responsibility and hers alone.

"I've been really busy these past few years, but this assignment gave me the chance to see you again, and I took it."

"And that's it? Just one old friend seeking out another at a time when it's convenient and would help your career?"

"It wasn't a casual decision." In fact, she remembered, it hadn't even been a decision at all. She'd had no control over the words she had spoken at the editorial meeting. But once they were out, she'd known they were right.

For a brief moment he took her face between his lean, elegant hands. "There's been a connection between us right from the first that defies labels,

Cate. Yeah, we're old friends, but we're also much more."

She waited until his hands dropped away, then drew a deep breath, summoning much-needed strength. "I can't tell you how special you are to me and always have been. I never wanted you to leave my life in the first place. I gave the Gallins fits because they took me away from you. I felt as if half of myself had been ripped out. But we *were* separated, and we've seen each other only sporadically since, and now you're talking about being together, being lovers." She shook her head. "It's too fast, Noah. I'm confused . . ."

"About what?" he asked impatiently. "And why? Everything is crystal-clear to me. For instance, I know that you and *only* you have the ability to make my fears more bearable just by being with me. I know that no one has ever stirred my heart the way you do. I know that I've never wanted a woman the way I want you right now. And you want me too, don't you? You've practically come apart in my arms the few times I've kissed you. *Think* what it's going to be like when we make love."

She held up a shaky hand. "It's not that *simple*, Noah. Nothing is. I mean, do you honestly believe that by going to bed with each other we'll solve all our problems."

"I can't think of one problem I have that wouldn't be solved by making you mine."

It was a powerful statement, and it fractured her resistance. To be Noah's . . . To be a part of his life . . . To wake up and go to sleep with this man who had been the most important person in her life. To be naked with him, to twist and strain against him . . .

He slid his hand beneath her hair so that his fingers circled the back of her neck. "We can go slowly. At least I can try. But you see, I have this problem. I can't seem to be around you without kissing you." He leaned forward and pressed a kiss, warm and hard, to her mouth.

She had to find a defense somehow, somewhere, she thought desperately. "I've got to have time to get used to this," she whispered.

He straightened away and looked down at her, his eyes dark as night. "Time has always worked against us, Cate. Don't take too long."

SIX

Cate had to go back to the pool to get her camera.

Her hopes that everyone had gone were dashed as she emerged onto the deck to find only Gloria and Bonnie missing. Dorsey, Santini, and Ian had arranged their lounge chairs close together, chilled bottles of water within their reach, and were deep in conversation. But when they saw her, they stopped talking and all three turned to stare at her.

"Where's Mac?" Santini called out without bothering to camouflage the blatant suspicion in his tone.

A giggle rose in her throat. She had the strongest urge to retort that she had hit Noah over the head and at that very moment the tide was taking his body out to sea. "The last time I saw him he was walking down the beach."

She reached the table and picked up the camera.

"Was he all right?" Ian asked.

"With the exception of a huge lump on his head," she muttered.

"*What?*"

"He was fine." A memory flashed through her mind of Noah as he walked away from her, a solitary figure with his hands shoved into the pockets of his jeans, the wind blowing fullness into his indigo shirt and rearranging the long waves of his ebony hair. She'd desperately wanted to go after him.

"Does Cy know that Mac's gone for a walk?"

She studied the three men as they were now, glaring at her with identical expressions of distrust. Their bodies were angled toward one another, but looked as though they were braced against her, three strong allies who saw her as a common enemy.

"Relax, guys. Your friend can take care of himself." Which was much more than she could say about herself at the moment, she thought wryly. On a sudden mischievous impulse she raised the camera and got off four quick shots. The shots would never make it into *Spirit*, but they would go into her own personal photo album. Three rich and famous men who saw her as a threat to them and those they loved. She couldn't help but find the situation funny; she'd never felt more innocuous in her life. With a smile at their slightly stunned faces, she headed toward the house.

On the path, she turned a corner and came face-to-face with Gloria, now dry and changed into a silk flowered-print sarong, all elegant bare arms and legs, her hair pulled back into a sleek braid.

"Hello." She fully expected the model to pass her by with a barely polite nod, but the other woman stopped.

"How did things go with you and Mac?"

"I beg your pardon?" She had heard Gloria perfectly, she simply needed an extra beat of time to decide what exactly Gloria was asking.

"You must have realized we saw him drag you away. And it was pretty obvious he was upset about something. Did he think you had started shooting too soon?"

"No, nothing like that. We simply had some issues we had to discuss."

"Really? You mean regarding the shoot?"

"Not exactly. I'm sorry, I don't mean to be evasive, it's just that some things are better left private. At least for now."

Gloria gazed at her for a moment. "I know what you think, Cate."

"Think?" She frowned. "About what ?"

"About my relationship with Dorsey."

"But I don't think anything at all, Gloria. It's none of my business."

"I know it's not, but that doesn't stop you from having an opinion, and you think I'm courageous to take him on."

Cate was too surprised to say anything. As a matter of fact, she *had* thought exactly that.

"You're an observant person, and the situation between Dorsey and me is painfully obvious." Gloria shrugged one bare shoulder. "I don't know if Dorsey and I will make it. There are places in that man I can't get to no matter how hard I try. But let me tell you, as tough as it is trying to have a relationship with Dorsey, I'd never even think about trying to have one with Mac. He's wonderful as a casual friend, but I've never met anyone as deep and as dark as he is."

"Why are you telling me this, Gloria?"

"I don't know. I've seen your work and I like it." She paused. "I guess I thought I should warn you."

Cate smiled. From the time she was five until she became an adult, people had done nothing else *but* warn her against Noah. The warnings hadn't done any good then and they wouldn't do any good now. "I appreciate it, Gloria. I really do. Thanks."

Gloria studied her a moment longer. "Something tells me I just made a mistake. You don't need a warning."

"Not really, but I appreciate it all the same. I'll see you later."

She managed to get into the house without encountering anyone else. She had a lot to think about and she wanted to be alone. In truth, what she really wanted to do was draw the drapes, climb into bed, pull the covers over her head, and stay for a few weeks. But never in her life had she done that, and she wasn't about to permit herself to do it now.

She hadn't checked into the office since her first day there. Reluctantly she picked up the phone and punched in the number.

As usual, Gary Winthrop answered. "Susan Hilcher's office."

"Hi, Gary. How are you? It's Catherine."

"Catherine!"

She smiled at his startled tone. "Yep, it's me. I'm basically just checking in to let you know—"

"Dammit, Catherine! I thought you were going to be checking in on a more regular basis. We don't even know exactly where you are, only that you're on McKane's estate. But we don't know where that is. We don't even have a number we can reach you at. Hell, Catherine—"

"Whoa, Gary. Calm down. I'll try to do better at checking in."

"What about a phone number?" His voice was so high, he was practically squeaking.

Spirit had always been a high-energy, high-stress place to work, she thought, amused, and quite obviously the stress was at a higher level than usual today. "Has Susan been giving you a rough time, Gary? You sound as if you're on your last nerve and that it's not doing too well."

"Nothing ever changes around here," he said, calm once more, his dry-edged humor back. "We're always on the edge of panic."

"I understand, and listen, I'd rather not give out Noah's phone number and address. There's no reason the magazine needs to stay in such close touch with me. You don't when I'm out of the country. Besides, if you do need to reach me, you can call Noah's office."

"Noah? What's this Noah business?"

"McKane." She hesitated. "Susan's not in, is she?"

"No, but you know she's going to want to talk to you. Can you call back in about an hour?"

She said a quick prayer of thanks that she wasn't going to have to talk with her boss. "Just tell her I called and everything's going great. Okay? Speak with you later."

"No, wait, Catherine—"

"Bye, Gary."

She hung up the phone, relieved that the call had been relatively painless. She really wasn't in the mood to hear Susan's exhortations regarding dirt and Noah.

Her skin felt tight, almost sore, her nerves edgy. She stripped and stepped into the shower beneath water turned as hot as she could stand it. The tingling spray pelted her, massaging her achingly tight muscles, but ultimately she found no relief.

Tension continued to build in her later that evening as everyone gathered for dinner. At the head of the table, Noah was silent and brooding, eating very little. Sensing his mood, his friends spoke more quietly and carefully than usual. Cate didn't speak at all.

Later everyone convened in the studio. Dorsey and Santini experimented with riffs, trading them back and forth. Then Noah picked up his guitar and started to play, and the other three band members stopped and listened.

He played brilliantly, searing his way through notes and chords, bending his guitar strings in a way no one else could copy, creating music that shimmered like fire and felt like passion.

He never once looked at her, but she knew that he was playing straight to her. She sat holding her camera, mesmerized by the hypnotic darkness of the music, captivated and enthralled by the compelling, heart-twisting emotions the music revealed. He was drawing her into a dark, private place where there was only him and his music, and its power reverberated against her senses, her skin, her soul.

Deeply disturbed, she left the studio early without taking a single shot.

When she awoke the next day, there were new storm clouds on the horizon, giant billowing clouds that piled on top of one another, darkening the sky, turning the day to lead gray. She eyed the clouds uneasily. They weren't the type that would simply blow out to sea. Those would come inland, bringing with them their fire and their rain, their sound and their fury.

Storms here were unseasonable this time of year, and she couldn't help but wonder if in her troubled state of mind she had personally conjured up this series of storms. Even as the ludicrous thought darted through her mind, she laughed at the amount of power she was ascribing to herself. She had to be losing it.

In an effort to dispel her troubled mood, she grabbed up her bag and camera and headed outside. Noah's estate spread over fifteen acres, most of it still in its natural state. She walked away from the house, away from the beach, away from the sight of the storm clouds.

A lone gull drew her attention as it flew over her head, back toward the storm. She turned and raised her camera, capturing the gull in graceful flight against the dark, boiling clouds—a fragile creature of nature pitted against the powerful force of nature. She felt an affinity with the bird and his coming struggle, and wondered what would happen to it when the storm made landfall. Would it survive?

On the surface, what Noah wanted from her seemed so simple. But the surface of anything could often be deceptive. His was an extremely complicated life. At any given moment his words and music were touching a million or more hearts around the world, thanks to the proliferation of radios, CDs, and tapes. He was no longer the protector he'd been to her when she was a child, nor was he the young man she'd had a crush on as a teenager. He was a man with a potent sexuality and magnetic power who could turn her inside out with just a kiss.

And he wanted more than a kiss from her, much more.

She topped a rise and came to a dead stop. Below her, Ian and Bonnie sat on a quilt in a small meadow blanketed with golden poppies. By some trick of light, a luminous glow bathed them, almost as if they had managed to find the one patch of sunlight that existed for miles. Bonnie was braiding a garland of flowers while Ian looked on, his expression gentle. They were so caught up in each other, they hadn't noticed her.

Cate had no intention of intruding, but instinctively she attached her long lens and framed the two of them. Just then Ian leaned toward Bonnie and said something, making Bonnie throw back her head and laugh. Cate snapped, capturing Bonnie's radiant beauty and Ian's fierce love for her.

Ian had told her not to take pictures of Bonnie, but she hadn't been able to resist this scene. Besides, the picture wouldn't be for *Spirit*, but rather a gift for them and their baby, this Juliette to come. Juliette's father might have a job that was radically different from any of her future friends' dads, but he would adore her, and she would come to cherish this picture of the happiness and love shared by her mom and dad when they had been waiting for her to be born.

Cate headed off in the opposite direction, her thoughts wistful. She would give anything to have a picture, any picture, of her birth parents. But after the accident that had taken their lives, there had been no relatives with the time or desire either to take her in and give her a home or to act to preserve the personal belongings of her parents. The lack of anything tangible of theirs had left her sad, longing for the anchor most other children took for granted.

And then one day ten-year-old Noah had come into her life, and at last she had something and someone to hold on to. At least for a while.

After that she had to learn to stand on her own.

The storm clouds were growing more forbidding, the sky darkening even more. The atmosphere was oppressive, the air so heavy she felt weighted down by it. There was no sight of Noah, and as each hour passed without seeing him, her nerves coiled a little tighter. She wanted to see him, she needed to see him. And as the dinner hour approached, her anticipation built. Her disappointment was palpable when he didn't appear in the dining room.

Gloria was also missing.

As candles glowed among a thicket of daisies arranged in the center of the table, Cate glanced around the table. The general mood seemed to be subdued.

"Where's Gloria?" she asked, addressing the question to everyone.

Dorsey, talking quietly to Ian, gave no indication that he heard her question, and it was left to Bonnie to answer. "She's going to be away for a few days. She's on an assignment."

"Really? Where?"

"Greece. Poor thing, she won't have a chance to see anything, just whatever she can glimpse from the cab window. Of course, she's been there a few times."

Cate glanced at Dorsey, but he gave no sign that Gloria's whereabouts affected him one way or the other. Gloria had said there were places in Dorsey she couldn't get to, no matter how hard she tried. Yet still she tried. Cate wished her well.

As the dinner progressed, she found her gaze straying to the head of the table time after time. Noah's absence nagged at her, and as dinner wound to a close, a needy ache for him formed inside her, growing as the minutes ticked by. "Will you all be working in the studio this evening?"

The three men looked at her as if, she thought, she had suddenly grown another head. At first she didn't think any of them would answer her. Finally, though, Santini broke the silence. "We're taking the night off."

His expression didn't encourage her to ask more questions, but she was in no mood to be acquiescent. "Is Noah taking the night off too?"

"I'm sure," Dorsey drawled in a tone that sounded as if it were made of ice chips, "if he had wanted you to have that information, he would have told you."

Her nerves snapped, and she gave a sound of exasperation. "For goodness sake, Dorsey, *lighten up*! I'm not here to hurt your beloved Mac." Ignoring the startled expressions, she pushed back from the table and left.

In her room she leafed through the books she had brought with her. Although they were by her favorite authors, she found that none of them looked interesting enough even to start. Agitated, she paced the bedroom.

Suddenly she came to a dead stop. *She had failed to ask Noah where she could set up a darkroom!*

She supposed that somewhere in the back of her mind she'd thought the matter would be easily solved, but it was telling that something so important to her work had slipped her mind until now.

It was also revealing that she had taken so few pictures. Normally by this time she would be well into the assignment. True, she had taken some, but few of them would make it to *Spirit*. They had been shots that had meant something personal to her, and ultimately were too private for public consumption.

Time crawled. She took a long bath but failed to relax. She slipped on the cotton chemise she slept in, then walked to the window, flinching every time she heard the faint rumbling of thunder. The rain was coming down hard, and every so often the blackness of the sky would split apart with lightning.

As the storm drew closer, her nerves worsened, crawling beneath her skin until she didn't think she was going to be able to stand it. She couldn't see the ocean, but she could hear it roar as wave after wave crashed with mighty power onto the shore.

Noah. His name kept coming to her, a punctuation to the fury of the storm. She was being foolish, she told herself. She had to stop thinking about him every time she heard thunder explode with a cracking boom. She had to stop worrying about him every time she saw lightning streak through the sky. She needed to heed her own words: Noah could take care of himself.

Thunder crashed over the house, rattling the windowpanes, making the lights flicker.

It was a habit, that was all, this need to go to him, to comfort him until the ferocity of the storm had passed and his heartbeat had slowed and returned to normal. But no matter what he said, he didn't need her anymore. Not for anything.

And she wouldn't go to him.

She opened the bedroom door and walked out. Blind instinct drove her along the darkened hallway in the direction of the den at the back of the house, the room where she'd first seen him the day she'd arrived.

She had no way of knowing for sure whether he would be there. She knew only that she had to check.

Then she heard the music. Someone was playing the piano, she thought with one breath, and with the next she knew it was Noah.

The music was intense, demon-haunted, layered with pain and suffering, fear and longing. It vied with the storm in its power, strength, and unearthly beauty. As she entered the room, thrills of both anticipation and anxiety rushed under her skin, and her blood drummed furiously through her veins.

Noah was sitting at the piano, one side of his face cast in darkness, the other side shadowed, almost demonic. His eyes were closed, his jaw set, his forehead beaded with perspiration, his ordeal etched in every line of his tensed body.

She had hurried down the hall, but now that she had him in sight she stood stock-still. The music and the storm were breaking over the house, and it sounded as if the world were splitting apart, but Noah never looked up. He played as though his life depended upon it, building the melody, layer by layer, like bricks in a wall, with the seeming intent to enclose himself in its safety.

Lamps cast pools of light into the darkness. She moved again, passing through one splash of light, then another, until she reached the piano. There she sat down beside him.

She could feel his tension as if it were her own, his fear as if it were a part of her. And in a way it was. The two of them hadn't been in this situation for years with him caught in the grip of his own private hell, with her trying to comfort him by her quiet presence. But it all came back to her as easily as if the last time had been yesterday.

The shirt he was wearing was unbuttoned, its sleeves folded halfway up his arms. Mesmerized, she watched the powerful muscles of his forearms knot with the effort of his playing.

Seeking to reassure him, she gradually edged closer until her thigh was pressed against his. The noise of the storm continued, but she wanted him to know that she was there with him, and she prayed that it would help. She willed the warmth of her body to touch him, her presence to gently entice him back to the world in which she lived.

He knew she was there, she thought. She could feel his awareness of her in the gradual calming of the music, the gradual relaxing of his muscles. He would be all right—another storm would soon be history.

Then the music slowed, by degrees turning sensuous, frightening her as much as it attracted her. Moments before, his music had exorcised his demons, now he was playing her a love song.

There were dangers in being so close to Noah, both physically and emotionally—she had known that for a long time—but suddenly there wasn't any fight left in her. She could resist him no longer.

Her emotions had been in a tangle over him since she was a little girl. She had loved him then with the purity of a child, had a crush on him as a mixed-up teenager, and been hurt by him as a woman with a tender heart. She didn't know if what she felt for him now was true love or not. She didn't know what to call what she was feeling, what it meant, its extent, its consequences.

There was only one thing she knew for sure. Tonight she hadn't been able to stop herself from trying to reach out to comfort him. And while there was a breath in her body, she would always go to him.

He brought his hands down on the keys, playing the final chord, and while the music still hung in the air around them, he turned to her, his eyes glittering with a dark pain.

"Are you all right?" she asked softly.

"I am now," he said, staring at her, trying by the very force of his will to absorb her presence into him.

Storms meant screams, blood, and death. Storms meant being all alone and desperately afraid. Storms meant nightmares and memories of the past. Except for those times when she came to him. Like tonight. Her scent, a light floral, had tickled at his senses, slowly awakening him from the living nightmare in which he descended during every storm, her warmth had filtered through his skin, through his pores, and into the tight muscle. She represented sanity to him; she always had.

"What were you playing?"

"My guts, my soul."

She nodded, understanding.

"I'm glad you came."

"I wasn't sure if I should. I wasn't sure if you were still afraid of storms."

"But you came anyway."

She raised one shoulder and let it drop. "I couldn't do anything else."

He rested his forearm against the top edge of the piano, his gaze on his hand as he clenched and unclenched it. "Now you know. Storms still terrify me." The admission wasn't easy for him.

"Then you still remember?"

"In vivid color. I'm haunted by it." His expression was grim as even now he had to fight against the memories, but she was the only person in the world to whom he would make such an admission. "During storms every single hellish moment comes back to me, and all I can do is try to get through it the best way I know how. The music helps drive it away. And you. You have that ability. You always have."

She reached for his hand, taking it and gently cradling it in hers. Slowly she straightened his fingers until his hand lay relaxed in hers. "It's time to do more than just get through it. It's time to forget it, Noah."

He looked back at her, the pain he was feeling showing clearly on his face. "Don't you think I've tried?"

"Remember when you told me that the past doesn't matter? Well, you were right, and you should apply it to yourself and forget the past."

"Don't you think I want to? Lord, Cate, I would if I could."

"You can."

"And have you decided that forgetting the past applies to us?"

She hesitated. The passion and intensity he'd poured into his music had been transferred to her. She felt it in the added warmth of her skin, in the quickening of her pulses. "I said I thought you were right."

"For my benefit, to comfort me."

"It's a comfort to me too, Noah."

His dark gaze searched hers. "The storm's over, Cate. Stay with me."

Some things never changed, she reflected. Her instinct was still to be with him during storms. The storm was over, but there was a new one building inside her. In one form or another, she'd always wanted him. Long ago, he'd become the shape of her world. Long ago, she'd given her heart and her soul to him.

He reached out and touched her cheek. "Please stay."

After all the years and all the pain, it was going to come down to this moment and two simple words. "I will."

He started to speak, but she put her fingers against his lips. "Don't make any promises that will be impossible to keep. Let's take this by steps, one at a time, starting with this one."

"If that's what you want."

"It is."

"What else do you want?"

"For you to say something that doesn't involve the past or anticipate the future."

"All right," he said, his voice low and thick. He lifted his hand to brush at the thin strap that crossed her shoulder. "What is this you're wearing?"

"It's the chemise I sleep in. I forgot I had it on."

Fresh hunger rose in him, an immediate, gnawing, basic hunger, an immense, almost critical craving that wouldn't stop or be satisfied with anything less than everything she had. A pulse throbbed at his temple as he realized that she was naked beneath the chemise. He pushed the strap from her shoulder, and the cotton slid down to expose the upper part of her breast.

She shuddered, as eager for his touch as she was her next breath of air. Just as she thought she wouldn't be able to bear the wait, he kissed her, hotly, deeply, and thoroughly, and his strong hands cupped her breast in a tender, extremely proprietary caress. It was a possession that rocked her to her toes. His tongue delved deep into her mouth to stroke in and out, driving her mad with pleasure. The kiss teased and tormented. It was erotic and completely carnal. And it made her wonder how she had lived as long as she had without him kissing her that way.

"I've wanted you for so long," he said so low his words sounded as if they were growled.

"Yes," she whispered, understanding, agreeing. Years had slipped through their fingers like so many grains of sand, years they could never regain. But no matter what else happened in their lives, they'd have this night, and nothing would ever take it away from them.

He stood up, dragging her with him, then pushed the piano stool away. He swept her into his arms and carried her into the next room. She didn't bother looking around her. The surroundings didn't matter. Only the man who held her was important.

For most of her life he had been the shape of her world, and now he was going to become her lover. It seemed so right. Somewhere before they were born it must have been written that this time would come. She had an inborn need to belong to him in this deeply intimate way, a primitive, raw kind of need that she couldn't deny, even if it was only for this night, this once.

No matter how much they might love each other, a future for the two of them wasn't feasible, but there was the present, and she was going to grasp it with both hands. She would give him everything that had been stored inside her for so many years. For the present she would be his and only his.

He placed her on her feet and then the wisp of cotton she had been wearing was gone, up over her head, and tossed aside. She trembled as she stood before him, this man of pain and passion, this man of fierce terrors and even fiercer desires, this man to whom she was about to give herself completely. His sexual possession would indelibly stamp her and make her his in a deeper, more complete way than ever before. And it was a stamp she would carry in her heart all the days of her life.

Perhaps a window stood open somewhere or a terrace door was cracked. She felt the rain-chilled air on her skin, but inside she was on fire.

Noah stared at her, unable to tear his gaze away. She was every song he'd ever written, every prayer he'd ever uttered. In the dimness of the room her skin carried the luster of satin. Her legs were long and sleek, her belly flat, her breasts round and high. "I'm going to explode with wanting you," he muttered.

With a bravery born of desire she snaked her arms around his neck and held him tightly. "Don't explode until you're as far inside me as you can get."

"*Cate.*" He shrugged out of his shirt, then yanked open the button on his jeans and slid down the zipper. Then he was sucking in another breath as her hands left his neck to slide down his chest to his waist.

"Let me," she whispered.

She took her time, drawing out the moment. She was increasing her own agony, but this was a moment too precious to rush. Slowly, carefully, she pushed his jeans past his hips. The discovery that he, too, was naked beneath his clothes halted her actions. He was magnificent, boldly and proudly erect, and the sight held her immobile and made her mouth go dry. Could a woman ever want a man as much as she wanted Noah? She didn't think it was possible.

It was he who moved, grasping her shoulders, walking her backward until she felt the bed against her legs. There was no resistance left in her anywhere. She lay back, sliding over the heavy silk spread beneath her, positioning herself for him, impatiently waiting.

Overpowered by his need for her, he went down to her. His blood rushing, his hand shaking, he touched her slender body, and he heard a soft cry tear from her throat. The rain was hitting against the windows, but tonight the storm was over for him. His head spun, as if he had drunk too much wine. His movements were jerky. He wanted her too badly. He'd been hungry too long. He was starved for her.

She pulled his head down and kissed him. It was like a dam breaking in him. He darted his tongue into the open cavern of her mouth and pressed against her softness. His hand stroked down, his fingers delved into her, finding her damp and tight. And he knew he couldn't wait much longer.

She began moving against his hand, moaning

softly. He whispered to her, encouraging her, discovering and pressing sensitive spots, listening to her moans. The sight, sound, and feel of her pleasure fed him. She'd always been there in his heart, in his soul, but he'd only dreamed of making her his.

He heard the muffled sound of thunder as it boomed in the distance, and he ignored it. He leaned down and skimmed his lips around one breast and fastened his mouth on its delectable peak. Gently tugging and sucking, he drank in her taste and inhaled her scent. She was velvet and perfume, femininity and sweetness, and most of all music—everything he loved most in the world. He would willingly die at this moment if it meant he could die in her arms.

As he felt her fingers tighten on his back, he raised over her and entered her with one powerful, sure stroke, feeling her contractions around him and hearing her cry out his name. Her body stiffened and she arched up to him. He drove into her again, his pelvis meeting hers. Then with a harsh groan and a fragile prayer on his breath he grasped her hips and let himself go completely, convulsing into her, trusting her as he'd never trusted anyone with the full and unguarded power of his heart and passion.

SEVEN

The dawn broke pearl gray and storm free. Cate slipped quietly from the bed, leaving Noah still asleep, his long, bronze limbs tangled in the sheets, his hard, muscular body at rest, his face half buried in a pillow. They had spent a spectacular night together, their lovemaking as electric and fiery as the storm that had come before it.

He hadn't been able to get enough of her, taking her time and again, her desperation for him equaling his for her. But the storm was over now, and a new day had appeared. She needed to get away from Noah, even if only for a while; she needed some emotional distance between her and what had happened between them in the night.

She made her way out of his bedroom and back to hers, where she took a shower, then dressed in taupe-colored slacks and a white cotton T-shirt with a scoop neck. Outside, she discovered that the storm had left the air cool, crisp, and clean.

The beach was her first choice, but the sun hadn't been up long enough to dry the sand. So with her camera in hand she strolled down the lawn to the terrace that skirted the edge of a small bluff and overlooked the ocean. Elegant old-fashioned wooden chairs filled with bright red cushions had been placed around a glass-and-wood table. She chose a chair and was grateful to find the cushion dry. Apparently the members of Noah's staff were even earlier risers than she.

The storm had dominated during the night, but with its passing the beach life had resumed. Three sandpipers braved the foam that curled in lacy patterns onto the sand, and gulls glided overhead on gentle air currents.

She studied them, wondering if one of them was the gull she had seen the previous day, the one whose predicament had reminded her so much of hers. She raised the camera and focused first on one, then on another, until she found a gull that caused her to stay with it. She wasn't certain why, but she thought she detected a certain valor in the way it soared against the blue sky, and she pressed the shutter button several times, capturing an "after" shot of a gull that had survived a storm and won its reward of a peaceful sky.

With a sigh she lowered the camera. The sky was clear. The sun was bright. A dream had come true last night. She and Noah had joined together in the most intimate way a man and woman could. She should feel on top of the world. So why did she still feel so uneasy?

"You brought your camera down here?"

She turned her head to see Noah, who was standing a few feet to her left, two cups of steaming coffee in his hands, hard, assured, and vitally attractive. It was impossible not to smile at him. So much for a chance to gain perspective, she thought wryly. "It's sort of a habit to have it in my hand." She nodded toward the coffee. "Is one of those for me?"

"Absolutely." He placed a cup on the table in front of her and the other one beside it, then lowered his head and pressed a brief but burning kiss to her lips. "Good morning," he said huskily.

"Good morning."

With a deep laugh he pulled a chair close to hers and dropped down beside her. "Tell me that's not shyness I hear in your voice."

The sip of coffee she took heated her insides just as his kiss had. "Okay, it's not shyness." But it *was* shyness. The shyness of a woman who had just spent the night learning how joyful and fulfilling sex can be when you're partnered with the man you care about deeply. Their coming together had been hot, sweaty, exquisitely slow, breathtakingly hurried, lustful, loving, and most of all bone-deep, soul-touchingly satisfying. And now she was facing her lover in the cold light of day, knowing that she had been changed forever, wondering if their lives would be any different, afraid that they wouldn't, and at the same time afraid that they would be.

Sipping his coffee, he settled back in the chair and studied her. "Why didn't you wake me up?"

"You were sleeping so soundly, I hated to disturb you. Besides, I needed some time to myself."

"I don't like the sound of that."

She smiled at him again. She couldn't help it. There was a chance—and a chance was all she was willing to acknowledge at that point—that she loved him. And with that chance came both peace and alarm. This new love would be different from the kind of love she had felt for him in the past stages of their life. It was a deeper, fully mature love, from a woman's heart. Unfortunately she had no experience with this kind of love, and she was alarmed by both the barriers and pitfalls she could see ahead of them. But then, there had always been barriers and pitfalls.

"Cate? You want to tell me what you're thinking?"

She nodded. "Okay, here it is. We were both vulnerable last night, Noah—"

"Stop right there." He set the cup down.

"You know you were. The storm—"

He made an impatient sound, his face somehow harder than before. "Okay, I'm vulnerable during a storm, we both know that. You've seen me through too many storms not to know. But why were *you* vulnerable?"

She had to pause for a moment and think how she wanted to reply. "I've been under a lot of strain lately."

"Why?"

She shifted uncomfortably in the chair, feeling incredibly foolish putting voice to the anxieties she had experienced the past few months. "It's nothing I can pinpoint exactly. Probably just my whole life-style. Too much travel, too much work, not enough sleep."

And shadows, a strange voice on the other end of the line in the dead of the night, belongings that seemed slightly out of place, things that went bump in the night . . .

"I wish you'd told me before now. Hell, I wish you'd come to me before now. Have you been sleeping since you've been here?"

"I've gotten more sleep," she admitted with a smile she hoped would coax him into a lighter mood.

He didn't return her smile. In fact, he looked more serious than she'd ever seen him. "Then let's get to what happened between us last night. Cate, if you hadn't come to me, I would have come to you . . . last night, tonight, tomorrow night. But count on it, I would have come." She shifted again, but his hand shot out and his long fingers curled around her arm, stilling her. "You might as well know that I already had made a private vow that you wouldn't leave me this time, at least not without our having resolved things between us once and for all."

"And you think our making love resolved anything?"

He leaned forward, his expression intense. "We went forward, Cate. We went *forward*. And I won't let us go back to the way we were—strangers who just happen to know each other better than anyone else in the world."

She looked at him, taking in the harsh lines and rugged planes of his face. They had never played games with each other, but as adults they had miscommunicated more than once. She wouldn't make that mistake again, not if she could help it. She had to try to be as up-front and as honest as she knew how. "I'm not trying to diminish what happened," she said softly. "It was wonderful."

A muscle moved along his hard jawline. "It was damned well spectacular."

She sighed, wishing she thought everything was going to be as easy as he obviously did, wishing she didn't feel this lingering sense of foreboding. "What do you want from me, Noah?"

"Not much," he said. "Just everything."

She was at a loss for words. She wanted him even now. The fact that he was so close was tantalizing to her. She wanted to reach out and touch him, to slide her hand around his neck and pull his head to her for another kiss. "Have you forgotten the assignment?"

"The assignment?" he asked blankly.

"*My* assignment for *Spirit*. I'm here only for the duration of the assignment."

"The hell you say."

"And I already have another assignment when I get back. It's for the anniversary issue of the magazine." As a reward for giving him this information, she received a stony stare. "What do you expect me to do, Noah? Give up everything I've worked so hard for and move in with you and become a groupie?"

"Groupie? Dammit, Cate, what in the hell are you talking about? I want you to be my wife."

She felt the breath leave her chest. "Wife?"

"I love you, Cate. You must know that, but if you don't, I'll say it again. *I love you.*"

She was frightened. Badly. The trouble was, she had no idea by what. She was being offered a miraculous gift, but there had never been any miraculous gifts in her life, and she couldn't help but be suspicious and unsettled.

Even as she silently cursed herself for not being able to easily reach out and take what he offered, she slowly shook her head. "I don't trust this. Nothing is this easy."

He took her hand. "Maybe this time it will be if we let it."

If we let it. Was it possible that loving Noah and being with him could really be that simple and easy? Was it possible that if she just relaxed and accepted his love as if he and she were two normal people, everything would be all right? She wasn't sure.

"I've never been able to hold on to anything, Noah. Not my biological parents, not my adoptive parents, not any of the relationships I tried to form in college with boys, not—"

"I understand, Cate," he said, interrupting because he knew what she was about to say. "Not me. But here I am. Again. Hell, Cate, don't you think I know the risks? My track record with people has been dismal. But one thing about it, you and I have always been able to give each other hope. And we have hope again, you and I. By asking for this assignment and coming here, by walking down that hall during the storm, by staying with me last night—you've given us hope again."

She understood what he was trying to say, but she wasn't sure she agreed. She might have been compelled to do all those things, and unconsciously she even might have been searching for hope. But she wasn't convinced she'd found it. She had a real sense of foreboding that she couldn't shake.

"You're a very public figure, Noah. I've always been a very private person."

"So what's your point? I may be a public figure, but you've got to admit that I've managed to stay private in most ways."

She nodded. It was true. "Frankly I don't know how you've done it."

"Just because I'm well known—"

"You're not just well known, Noah. You're *idolized* by millions."

"*Idolized* is a pretty strong word and completely beside the point. Some things are too precious or too private to share, and I never have. You fall into the former category, my past falls into the latter."

Her concerns were legitimate, she knew, but she also realized that in many ways she was quite simply, plain-out fretting. But it didn't matter. The fact remained that she was genuinely worried. "And so what now? What happens when it becomes known that you and I are seeing each other?"

"Dammit, Cate, I want us to do a hell of a lot more than see each other."

She did too, so badly she was positively vibrating with the need. But in her experience, life simply didn't fall into place that neatly, like a jigsaw puzzle where all the pieces fit as you wanted them to and there were no extras for you to worry about.

"You know what I mean. Noah, you live in front of the camera. I live behind it. Being with you would put me in the spotlight, and I would hate that. I'm used to being invisible."

"Do you see any spotlights now? It's just you and me here."

She wrapped her arms around herself in an attempt to control a shudder. "I know I'm being silly, but—"

"Cate, you've got to know that I would do everything in my power to protect you, to make sure that nothing of my public life touched you, if that's the way you want it. All that's important is you and me."

He made so much sense. . . . "I know that you're right, but—"

"Then what's bothering you? Tell me. You're spooked. In fact, I've never known you to be this spooked. What is it? Is it me?"

She shook her head, unable to explain it. "I feel so silly, because I'm not even sure why. It's a feeling I can't seem to shake." She paused and focused on him, *really* focused on him—on his gleaming ebony hair that tumbled over his dark eyes, on the strength and love for her she saw in his face. "You're proposing we go from nothing to everything in what seems like a split second."

"We've had nothing for too damned long, Cate."

Words, emotions, passions—they had all been damned up inside her for so long. What would happen if she let them go? Would they engulf and destroy her? On the other hand, would she survive if she didn't let them go?

"You know," she said slowly, "in some ways I've been only existing during the years we've been apart."

He exhaled a long, shaky breath. "I feel the same way."

Leaning toward him, she touched his face with a loving caress. "Okay, then. Okay. This is the deal. Don't ask me about love right now. I need time to sort out some things. And I don't know about marriage. Being your wife is something way beyond my comprehension at the moment. But we can try being together, taking one day at a time, one hour, and if that doesn't work, we'll take it one minute at a time. We owe it to ourselves. To do any less would be cheating ourselves, and no matter what I'm feeling, I can't do that."

He reached out for her, triumph and happiness in his expression. "Cate—"

There was a loud *thump*. In her peripheral vision she saw the stuffing of the pad on the chair directly across from her shred and the wood behind it splinter. An instant later there was a sharp crack. "What—"

Almost immediately it happened again. The stuffing shredded, flying everywhere, and the top of the chair disappeared as it came apart. Then another sharp crack sounded.

Noah grabbed for her, pulled her out of the chair, shoved her to the ground, and came down on top of her, covering her body with his. "*Cy!*"

Confused, she tried to get up. "Noah—"

"Stay down," he ground out harshly. "Don't move."

In the distance she heard Cy cursing and shouting orders. Then the siren went off as it had a few nights before. She stiffened.

"Don't worry," he muttered. "That's only to alert everyone. We have to do it, but I haven't heard another shot. I hope the son of a bitch doesn't get scared off. I want him caught."

Noah's body pressed heavily down on her. The grass was damp beneath her. She thought she could feel each individual blade that was crushed beneath her arm. She heard a roaring sound in her ears. Ice had entered her veins. "Somebody's shooting at us." She said the words aloud, trying to make the idea more real so that she could accept it and then take appropriate action, if there was such a thing as appropriate action for being shot at. "Somebody's shooting at us." It didn't sound any more real to her than it did the first time she said it.

"*Me*, honey," he said grimly. "They're shooting at *me*."

Her mind was working faster than it had ever worked in her life, and at the same time she couldn't seem to get it to process the information. "You?"

That didn't sound right to her. It *couldn't* be right.

It had never once occurred to her that his life could be in danger. He gave pleasure to millions of people. Why would anyone want to kill him? It didn't make sense. But there was no doubt someone *was* shooting at them.

"Lord, Noah, get off me! Get to some kind of cover! *Protect yourself!*" She pushed against him, frantically trying to get him to move.

"Stay still!"

She heard feet running toward them, then Cy's tense, rough voice. "Come on. The shots came from that rise about a quarter of a mile south of here. Stay with me, and I'll get you back to the house."

Noah pushed himself up from the ground, and with his hand around her arm brought her up with him and barked a terse order to her. "Keep close."

Two other men Cate had never seen before materialized around them, forming a protective wall. Noah pulled her against him and urged her

into a run. They didn't stop until they had reached
the house.

Cy motioned for the two men to guard the
doors, then turned back to Noah. "Stay away from
the windows. I'll be back."

"Wait! What about the band?"

Cy glanced back at him, his usually sleepy eyes
sharply alert. "I have someone with each of them.
They'll be fine. It's you I'm worried about. Be sure
you stay inside until I've found out what the hell
happened."

As soon as they were alone, Cate grasped Noah's
arm. "Are you all right?"

He nodded, anxiously scanning her for any signs
of harm. "I'm fine. What about you? You're not
hurt, are you?"

She shook her head. "No. *Noah*, I thought your
property was *secure*."

"The immediate grounds around the house are.
But I've got fifteen acres here. I've never seen the
need to wire all fifteen acres."

She absorbed that information. How ironic that
she had felt so safe here during her stay. "But why
would anyone want to shoot you?"

His mouth thinned into a grim line. "Name
a reason, and you'll have it. It can run the
gamut, all the way from a fan thinking that a
voice spoke to him and told me I should die,
to someone thinking it's been too many days,

months, years, whatever, since I've put out an album."

She stared at him, suspicious. "Has this happened before?"

With a hand on her back he guided her deeper into the room and away from the wall of windows. His movements were almost nonchalant, but she could feel the tension in his hand against her back.

"You mean, has anyone ever shot at me? No. No one. But there've been letters over the years. Or at least that's what Cy tells me. I've never looked at them."

She tried to absorb this new information. Tried and completely failed. "Is it widely known that you live here? I mean, can the average person figure out that this is where you live?"

"I have several homes. Their location is not information that's readily available, but it's also not a secret. Most people who want to find out badly enough can. Hell, a well-placed question here and there to a local resident can pretty much pinpoint the place, especially if I've been in residence for a while, like I have been this time."

She was horrified. She'd always pictured Noah as safe. *She'd* been the one who traveled the world alone and unprotected. *She* was the one who had felt the foreboding. Was this its fulfillment?

When they reached the farthest point away from the windows, he stopped. Blowing out a long breath, he raked his fingers through his hair, then began to pace. "I'm sorry, Cate. I'd give anything if this hadn't happened. God, what if you'd been hurt?"

Her eyes followed him. "I wasn't."

"But what if you had been? What if one of those bullets that had been meant for me had hit you?"

His eyes were darker than she had ever seen them. "What if it had hit you?" The mere thought caused her pain.

He came to a stop a few feet away from her and looked at her a moment, his eyes glittering with some private torment. "Maybe you were right."

"About what?"

"I think you were right to be cautious about being with me."

Something had changed with him, shifted. She could hear it in his voice, see it even in the way he held his body. He was closing up right in front of her, and in many ways it frightened her more than those bullets had. "What are you talking about?"

He shook his head, his expression bleak. "You know what? You should go to your room and stay there until Cy gives us the all-clear." He took a few steps away from her, putting space between them.

She had the strange sensation the space between

them was more like miles than steps. "What's happening here, Noah? What are you doing?"

"I'm trying to keep you safe." He waved his hand toward the wall of glass. "You'll be safer in your room."

"If I will, you will be too. Come with me."

"No. I'm going to stay here until Cy comes back."

"Then I'm staying with you."

"Stop being stubborn, Cate."

"You can call me any name you like, Noah, but I'm staying." She chose a chair and sat down. "And I'm asking you again, what's going on? Before those bullets hit, I had just agreed that we owed it to ourselves to try to make what we have together work."

He shook his head. "You were right to be hesitant. There are a lot of obstacles—your career, for instance."

"I can still work. I'll simply have to commute. *Spirit*'s offices are only about an hour away. And I'll have to travel some, but then, so will you. It'll be hard at times, but so is anything worthwhile, or so I hear."

Noah glared at her. She stared back. Minutes passed—suspenseful, painful, eternal minutes. Between them the silence was dense, like a wall, solid and impenetrable. Many times Cate started to speak, but stopped herself. An awesome torment etched Noah's face that she couldn't decipher.

Then Cy returned. "The bastard got away." He walked to Noah and held out his hand. Two spent cases lay in his palm, along with several blades of grass tied into neat knots. "I found these exactly where I thought I'd find them, on that hill south of the terrace about a quarter of a mile away. He'd spent his time knotting blades of grass. These were only a few of them. They were everywhere. It looks like he'd been up there for hours, waiting for you."

A chill settled onto Cate's skin. "He?" she said, unable to remain silent. "You know it was a man?"

Cy spared her a glance. "I'm just about positive. A woman would stab a man or poison him. She'd even shoot him between the eyes if she were in a rage or protecting someone she loved. But sitting on top of a hill for hours in wet grass, propping up a high-powered rifle and staring through a scope, isn't a woman's style."

She was trying hard to understand. "Who do you think it could have been? Noah mentioned some letters he'd been getting."

"It was more than likely some loyal but deranged fan. The person certainly wasn't a professional." He sent a disapproving glance Noah's way. "The way you threw yourself on top of Catherine left you completely exposed, and he still missed." He paused as he absorbed Noah's stony demeanor. "You didn't like that? You're going to like this even less—I'd like you to play it cool for the next few days. Either I or one of the boys will escort you to and from the studio, and you're to stay away from the beach."

"Dammit, Cy."

Cy held up his hand. "I know, it sucks. But better safe than sorry. The police are already here. They'll want to talk to both of you, but it shouldn't take long."

"Cy?" Cate said.

"What?"

"My camera. It's still on the table."

"I'll see that you get it."

The police came and talked to Cate and Noah separately, and as soon as they left, Noah disappeared.

Cate chose not to try to find him. She was bewildered and hurt by his withdrawal from her. She did go looking for Cy, though, and inquired about a room she could use as a darkroom. As she'd hoped, he was able to help her, and she spent the afternoon setting it up and developing film.

That evening a fog crept in off the ocean. Cate sat through dinner with very little appetite, but everyone around her behaved as though nothing unusual had happened. There was joking and laughing, and Noah sat at the head of the table, appearing to enjoy it all.

After dinner everyone adjourned to the recording studio, and the only sign that anything out of the ordinary had taken place that day was that several guards accompanied them.

To keep her sanity, Cate began taking pictures. She finished a roll of color film, decided to concentrate almost exclusively on Noah, and loaded the camera with black and white film. The lighting wasn't good, the framing was off, but the magic was there. Noah made the magic, lost in his music, unaware of anything or anyone.

He wasn't simply playing the guitar, he was setting it on fire with his emotions. He wasn't merely singing, but, rather, bringing up his soul and sharing it

The pictures, once developed, would not reveal the sound or the words. They would be a silent, still record, in black and white, but she knew instinctively he would practically jump off the pages of the magazine. And his wizardry would come through in the simple things—the commanding, natural way he held the guitar, as if it were an extension of himself, his assured stance with his feet planted and his body bent to the guitar, and lastly, his intense, almost passionate expression.

It would all be there—the magic of Noah.

EIGHT

There was no storm, but Noah couldn't rest. In his darkened bedroom he stood by an open French door, staring out at the clear night, but he wasn't seeing anything. His sight was turned inward, and he was hearing the sounds he always heard whenever a storm came, as it had last night, or when he was upset and troubled, as he was now. Sounds he'd been trying to forget for over a quarter of a century. The sounds of the nightmare that recurred periodically.

He'd played his heart out tonight, trying to get lost in the music, trying to escape the nightmare. But the violence that morning had brought it all back. His hand clenched and unclenched as he remembered. . . .

A scream pierced the loud noise of the storm that raged around the small house. Noah, eight years old

and gripped by fear, sat straight up in his narrow bed.
"Mom?"

There was no answer. He knew his mom often
brought a man home with her. Sometimes he heard
noise. But . . .

There was another scream and another until the
screams merged with the storm—in his mind, pain and
fury becoming one.

Heart nearly beating out of his small chest, he scrambled out of bed and ran toward the sounds. Just inside the
door of the living room, he stumbled against something
and fell hard to his knees. Bewildered, he glanced behind
him and saw that he had tripped over the table lamp. Why
was it lying like that on the floor, its shade tilted crazily?
He looked around. Tall, distorted shadows danced eerily
across the wall. Thunder boomed.

"Lord in heaven, stop! Please, stop!"

It was his mom! He sprang to his feet just as he heard
the dull, thudding sound of a fist hitting flesh, then a
sickening crunch as bone gave way. Her pleas stopped.

Fully awake now, he hurled himself at the back of the
man who was beating his mom. Without releasing her,
the man swung a mighty fist and connected with Noah's
face, knocking him across the room. Pain exploded and
engulfed his slight body as his head hit the wall.

"Run, Noah, run!" His mom was calling to him,
but then he heard the unmistakable sound of fist
hitting flesh as the man delivered another blow
to her.

He did run. He ran into his mom's bedroom, to the bedside table. Jerking open the drawer, he reached for the gun she kept there.

He had to help his mom!

Seconds later he was back in the living room. The gun was heavy, but he held it with both hands, and he aimed it straight at the man.

"Stop hurting my mom!"

Lightning stabbed the room. ~~Impossibly~~ loud thunder cracked overhead. He could no longer hear his mom screaming.

The man turned and started toward him, his face distorted with rage. Noah pulled the trigger, the force of the discharging gun propelled him backward, and he lost his balance and fell. But he still saw the man grab his chest and crumple to the floor. And he saw the blood . . . on the man . . . on his mom.

Then he began to scream.

He had held his mother's dead body in his arms, whispering to her over and over again, he remembered. *"Mom, wake up. Mom, please wake up."* But she hadn't. When the police arrived, they had to pry him away from her.

And ever since that night he'd been trying to get the sound of the screams and thunder out of his head.

"Noah?"

His eyes squeezed shut. *Cate.* The one person he didn't want to see. He'd chased the nightmare away before. He would again. But his strength where Cate was concerned went only so far.

"Noah, something's wrong. What is it?"

"Go away, Cate."

"No. Not until you tell me what's wrong."

Slowly he turned and looked at her. She was wearing the flowered dress again, the one she'd worn the first night she was there. She looked very fragile, very frightened and pale. Of course she did. She'd been *shot* at today—because of him. He gave a barely audible curse. "Dammit, go away."

He dropped down into a big overstuffed chair that was positioned in a moonlit pathway and covered his eyes with his hand. But even though he could no longer see her, he could sense her presence. Her scent invaded his senses, a lovely light floral that did strange things to him, disturbing, interfering, disorienting. Her warmth came to him, touching him, coiling inside him, making him want her.

He opened his eyes. She was kneeling in front of him, the skirt of her dress in a flowered circle around her, her hair in shining soft disorder around her lovely face, her expression patient and concerned.

"I'm not going away."

He groaned. "God, but you're contrary. When I want you to stay, you fight me, and when I want you to leave, you won't."

"*Talk* to me about contrary. This morning you told me you loved me and asked me to be your wife, and then you proceeded to ignore me."

His lips quirked and he rubbed his face tiredly. "You're underestimating yourself, Cate. A man would have to be dead to ignore you."

She eyed him calmly. "It's because you were shot at, isn't it?"

He gestured vaguely. "It's amazing how getting shot at will make a man come face-to-face with his own mortality."

"So getting shot at has made you rethink asking me to marry you? Is that what you're telling me?"

"Actually, I believe my exact words were *go away*."

She gave an abrupt, mirthless laugh. "You'll forgive me if I'm a little slow in responding, Noah. It's not every day I'm proposed to and then told to go away by the same man."

"As I recall, you rejected my proposal."

His soft drawl raked across her nerves. "If that's all you remember, then you have a lousy memory. I said I wanted to try and you were reaching out to me just as the first bullet hit."

He closed his eyes, hearing again the thud as that bullet slammed into the chair across from her. Every time he thought about how close it had come to hitting her, he was sickened.

"Talk to me, Noah."

He opened his eyes and exhaled a long, weary breath. "You want to talk? Okay, we'll talk. Did you know that you were the only person who trusted me when we were growing up?"

"That can't be true."

He nodded somberly. "It is. Oh, the social workers tried to connect with me, but I could sense their unease. Looking back on it, I think they were good people. It's just that they didn't know what to make of me."

Cate spread her hands. "That's because you would never talk to them."

"I didn't have anything to say to them."

"But you talked to me."

"Yes," he murmured, his gaze fixed steadily on her face. "I talked to you. Your skin was baby soft, and you smelled like innocence. And you'd look at me with those big green eyes of yours as if you thought I hung the moon."

A trace of a smile curved her lips. "I guess back then I thought you did."

He gazed at her mouth, at the smile, for a moment. "The fact is, I killed a man when I was eight years old, and people looked at me as being very different from other kids."

"If they did, I'm sure it was because they were curious and felt sorry for you."

"You didn't look at me like that, and I felt a huge responsibility toward you, especially as I grew older, to protect you from me."

"From *you*? Why?"

"I had *killed* a man, Cate. How do you think that made me feel?"

"I know how it made you feel," she said quietly. "You were tormented by it and have been ever since."

"Yeah, but I'm really talking more than that. When I was young, especially during my teens when I was struggling so hard to find my way and become a man, I couldn't help but wonder if there was something inside me that was predisposed toward violence."

Her brow pleated. "But that's *nonsense*."

"I didn't think so then. I knew that I had killed a man, and I knew that I had never met one other person, not one, who could say the same. In my mind that put me in a pretty select group of one."

"Yes, but—"

"I had done it once. Who's to say I wouldn't do it again? You were the one person in the world who didn't think I was odd or different. I needed you, but I also had to protect you. From me."

She was flabbergasted. "You don't still believe that, do you?"

"What happened that night—to my mother, to that man who beat her to death—is part of who I became. That violence was permanently imprinted on me. But I grew out of believing I would hurt you physically in some way. By the time I was out of my teens I understood I'm just not capable of violence unless someone I love is in danger."

"Of course you're not. I wish you'd shared this with me back then. I would have told you that."

"You did tell me that, time and time again, but not in words. You told me by the things you did: the way you'd sneak into my bed during a storm; the way you'd reach for my hand whenever you were unsure about anything; the way you'd smile at me. You were never afraid of me." A ghost of a smile lit his face, then was gone again. "You were good for my soul, Cate."

She eyed him with the caution of someone who knows the other shoe has yet to drop. "So why do I think there's a *but* about to come?"

He rolled his shoulders. "I think you should go back home tomorrow. You should be able to find enough in the shots you took tonight to make your layout. It doesn't have to be as big as you originally planned."

Two thoughts entered her mind at once: He *had* been paying attention to her in the studio. And he was once more trying to protect her. "Are you afraid the man who shot at us today will try again? Is that it?"

He exhaled a long breath and rubbed a hand across his face. "I try really hard to control my surroundings and my life. The need to control it probably started that night when I was eight and picked up that gun. It was the only thing I could do at the time. Over the years—as I've gotten more successful and have accumulated money along with a kind of power—controlling my life has gotten easier. But my ability goes only so far, and this morning is a perfect example of something I can't control. The next time a bullet comes my way, if there is a next time, I don't want you anywhere around."

She stood in a sudden blur of limbs and flowered cotton until she was standing in front of him, looking down at him, her green eyes glinting with anger. "That's the most selfish thing I've ever heard you say, Noah. *You* don't want this. *You* don't want that. Well, guess what? I don't care what *you* want."

"Cate—"

"No, you listen to *me*. Last night, after years of almost-but-not-quite connecting with each other, you and I made love for the very first time. This morning you asked me to marry you. Now, granted that part scared me a little, and I couldn't and still can't make any promises to you about marriage, but I told you I wanted to give us a chance. After the years we've spent apart, that's a huge step forward. And nothing has happened to change my mind—especially not that creep of a guy on the hill, whoever he is. I still want to try, more than ever."

He was convinced that if he listened closely enough, he would be able to hear himself breaking apart on the inside. No matter how much he wished, he couldn't let himself reach out and take what he so desperately wanted. The only other person he'd ever truly loved with all his heart was his mother, and he'd watched her being killed right before his eyes. He had no intention of the same thing happening to Cate.

He wanted her badly, but not badly enough to put her life in danger. A part of him would die when she left, but as long as he knew she was alive somewhere in the world, he'd be okay.

"I'm not willing to risk your life, Cate, and that's that."

"Dammit, Noah, you're infuriating. It's my life. *I* decide when, where, and how I risk it."

"In this case I don't believe you're thinking as clearly as you might."

"Oh, and you are? Cut out the macho crap, Noah. This is me you're talking to, remember? Besides, I'd like you to tell me how you propose I leave you and get on with my life, when all the while I'd be worried out of my mind about you."

"You'll manage."

"You're wrong, so forget it. I'm staying."

He leaned his head back and closed his eyes once more, but he could still see her as if her image had been permanently etched on the inside of his lids. And he knew he'd see her no matter what. Always.

He opened his eyes. "I've decided to cancel the shoot."

She should have been prepared for it, but she wasn't. "You can't do that."

"Yes, Cate, I can. Remember the agreement we made the day you came here? You agreed that if I became uncomfortable at any point, you'd stop. Well, guess what? I'm *damned* uncomfortable."

"But not because of my work."

"It doesn't matter why I'm uncomfortable. Only that I am." Both his voice and expression were flint hard.

"I *realize* that you're used to people doing exactly as you say, but I'm not one of those people. What you're asking doesn't make sense."

"Probably not," he drawled. "In fact, I'm sure you're right. I seem to have real unreasonable feelings on this matter, and you're stuck with them."

"Well, see, that's where you're wrong. I'm not. I can do exactly as I want, and I don't want to leave. Noah, if I leave here now, you and I may never have another chance."

"I'd rather you be alive without me than stay with me and be killed."

She felt like screaming, and in a minute, she thought grimly, she just might. "And what *I* want doesn't matter?"

"You want to be dead?"

She was going to slap him any second, she thought.

"I would like you to leave now. I'm tired, and I'd like to get some rest."

She stared down at him, frustrated, furious. "You slept longer than I did last night, Noah. You can't be that tired." He didn't answer.

Her pride asserted itself. She tried to tell herself that if he didn't want her with him, she didn't want to be here. Baloney. Her heart was asserting itself with even more power than her pride. He was trying to protect her, and losing her temper would do no good. She might fault his reasoning, but she couldn't change his mind. No, she was simply going to have to change her tactics.

Slowly she lowered herself onto his lap until she was straddling him, her legs on either side of him.

"What are you doing?" he asked gruffly.

"What I'm doing is *not* going away."

"Cate—"

"Hush now." She put her fingers to his lips, silencing him. "You've said everything there is to be said. We're not going to agree on this. So let's not talk for a while."

He put his hands on her arms as if he were going to push her away, but she bent her head and replaced her fingers with her lips. She brushed her mouth across his with the lightest of touches, then back again. The fire in the pit of her stomach was immediate, as was Noah's response. She could feel the pressure of his sex between her thighs increase as he began to harden. Encouraged, she continued, settling more of the weight of her body on him and deepening the kiss. Her breasts swelled against his chest, her nipples hardened, and she began to ache for him.

She was being shameless, she thought dimly. But she'd gone without him for so long, and her appetite and hunger knew no bounds. *Surely* he had to feel the same way.

She took his face between her two hands, making him look at her. "After being with me last night, do you really want to be alone tonight?" He tried to shake off her hold, but she held fast. "The *truth*, Noah. Tell me the truth. I want you. Don't you want me?"

Her question stabbed through him with a white-hot heat. Lord, just having her sitting on his lap was warping his senses, his reason. He gripped her waist tightly, digging his fingers into the soft flesh at her waist. "You want the truth?" he asked, his voice rough and gritty. "Okay, the truth is I can't bear the thought of spending a minute without you being at my side, much less a night."

Hope blossomed in her. "Then I can stay."

His brow moistened with sweat, and his lungs felt as if lack of air had scorched them through and through. He was hurting body and soul. His gut was in knots. Desperately he tried to gather the remnants of his control. "No, Cate, you can't. This is the way it has to be. What happened this morning made last night a mistake. I'm a selfish bastard in a lot of ways, but not where you're concerned. I want you to go back to your room, pack, and leave first thing in the morning."

If she had believed that he was sending her away because he didn't want her, she would have gone immediately. But as she stared down at him, she saw the desire in his eyes and the agony on his face, and she knew a flash of victory. "I can change your mind."

"Don't even try."

"Why? Are you afraid I'm right?"

"It'll be a waste of your time."

"I've got time to waste." She lowered her head and kissed him again. Her lips were soft on his, but nevertheless sure and sweet as they set about learning his mouth in a whole new way. She could feel him trying to hold back, feel his tension in the bunched muscles of his legs and arms. But she wasn't discouraged.

"Come on, Noah. You know you want this as much as I do. Let go . . ."

She moved her hips over him, and at the same time slipped her tongue between his lips and discovered his, both velvet and rough. Pockets of heat ignited all over her body, and she leaned into him, pressing her breasts against his chest, delving her tongue deeper into his mouth.

"Let go," she murmured again.

A low, uneven sound rumbled from his chest. His whole body was tensed against responding, but he couldn't stop himself. He was no saint. He was only a man who wanted her so badly, he feared he might rip apart with the pain of it.

He reached beneath her skirt and with one hard pull tore her panties. Almost simultaneously her hands went to his zipper. Eagerly she reached for him, then released him and closed her fingers around him.

"Damn you, Cate." Her name was a sound created somewhere between heaven and hell.

He lifted her and brought her down again, impaling her on his hard length. Pure, sharply exquisite pleasure, the likes of which he'd never felt before, shot all the way through him. Grasping her hips, he rocked her on him. She was so small and slim, but her contractions were so strong. She made him burn and want. He'd never known anything like this storm of desire she made him feel. He'd always loved her, but now he found himself swamped by his feelings for her. All those years of being alone in a crowd, of the constant grind of touring and performing, all those years of wanting her with him, but not having her. And now she was with him and he was in her, and he didn't think he could ever do without her again. Not ever.

He felt her stiffen, then arch against him with a joyful cry as her release came. Then he was gritting his teeth as his own climax gripped him, hard and powerful, and he went crashing over the edge. She collapsed against him, gasping for air. He held her close, waiting for his heartbeat to slow, smoothing his hand down the damp skin of her back, soothing her, him, knowing he had never in his life experienced such deep emotional pleasure. After a while he lifted her and carried her to bed.

She cuddled against him and drifted off to sleep, thoroughly satisfied, thoroughly exhausted, content that she had gotten them past the latest obstacle.

"I still think you should go."

It was the first thing Noah said to her the next morning, and Cate was both stunned and hurt. They had made love several times in the night. Their hunger for each other was insatiable. He had rarely allowed her to leave his arms. They had been as close as two people could get, two lovers joined as one. But now he wanted her to leave.

"The subject is closed, Noah." She sat up, swung her legs over the side of the bed, and wrapped the top sheet around her.

He pushed himself up in bed, piling pillows behind him for support. "Are you staying because of your assignment or because you love me?"

"I could say both and be completely truthful."

"We've loved each other all our lives, but that's not the kind of love I mean."

"I'm staying because I'm contrary. Isn't that what you said last night?"

Angry and annoyed, she stood, taking the sheet with her, leaving him sprawled naked on the bed. Last night she had given herself to him without reserve, and it put her distinctly out of sorts to be told to leave after the hours they had spent making love. Strolling around the room, she studiously avoided looking at his naked form. "You know, don't you, that if I had a gun right now, I'd be tempted to shoot you myself? I thought we'd settled whether or not I'm going to stay, which, by the way, I am."

His lips quirked as his gaze followed her. He'd had to try one more time to get her to leave, but Lord, he was grateful she refused to go. "Then if you're staying, I want you to promise to do exactly as Cy says. No more long walks by yourself like you took the other day."

She looked back at him. "Nothing gets by you, does it?"

"Not much where you're concerned. Open the bottom two drawers of the chest."

"What?"

"Just open them."

She cast him an odd glance, but knelt to the task and discovered the same thing in both drawers— leather-bound notebooks that seemed to contain every picture she'd ever taken that had been published. In effect, it was a record of her career. "How in the world did you get all these?"

He smiled. "One of my secretaries has collected all of those for me. For years she's pored through various publications, but mainly *Spirit*. She may have missed a few, but I don't think many."

"Wasn't she curious about why you wanted them?"

"Probably, but she never asked. As for me, I wanted a record of how you were doing and where you had been." He paused. "I've been very proud of what you accomplished, Cate."

Tears filled her eyes. "Oh, Noah." Her tone was sad and regret filled.

"Don't," he said softly. "Don't try to look back and think of what might have been. Fate has given us a rare opportunity by bringing us together again. We need to take care and not blow it this time."

Her gaze turned thoughtful. "Does that mean you'll stop asking me to leave?"

"I was doing it for your sake, not mine."

"Then for my sake, stop."

The smile he gave her was without darkness or reserve. "Come back to bed, Cate."

Not yet, she thought. She had one more thing to say to him.

"I love you, Noah. I love you with all my heart. I love you now, I loved you long ago, and I'll love you forever."

He held out his arms to her, and she went to him.

NINE

"The tickets for your concert went on sale this morning and sold out in under fifty minutes."

The speaker was an energetic, smartly dressed man, probably in his late thirties, Cate judged. He had been introduced to her as Noah's manager.

"Good."

It was the only comment Noah made, the only indication that he was pleased thousands of fans had jammed the phones and stood in lines for hours just for the chance to get a ticket to see him and the band perform.

It was the middle of the afternoon, two days after someone had tried to shoot Noah, and a large group of people had gathered in the den. Besides Noah, his manager, his lawyer, and the members of the band, there was Bonnie and several people from Noah's office staff. They had shown up with files and papers for both Noah and the band to go over. Even Cy was perusing a sheaf of papers that they had brought him.

Noah's office was located in downtown Los Angeles, but it was clear to Cate, even though nothing had been said, that the staff had come to him so he didn't have to leave the estate. The reason gave her chills.

Studying the activity that swirled around Noah, Cate felt far removed from it all. There was so much she didn't know about his life, so much he didn't know about hers. Their relationship was intimate on a great many levels, yet unfamiliar on so many others.

How had Noah put it? Two strangers who just happened to know more about each other than anyone else in the world. And now they were trying to attempt what currently seemed to her to be something almost impossible—to be together. But they loved each other. Surely that had to count for something.

Noah initialed a legal document, handed it back to his manager, then turned to Cy. "I'd like to see those letters you're looking at when you're finished. From now on, you're to let me know about anything that appears even remotely suspicious or threatening."

Cy shrugged. "Sure, if that's the way you want it." He leaned over and handed him the papers.

"These are all the crank letters we've received in the last six months, and I can't find anything that's abnormally suspicious in any of them. They seem to me to be just your regular, everyday discontents."

Santini pushed a pair of reading glasses atop his tan-colored hair and gave a half-smile. "Maybe the guy who took those shots at you isn't the letter-writing type, Mac."

Dorsey gave a short, cynical chuckle. "Right. Besides, there's something so much more *personal* about a bullet, don't'cha think?"

"When you care enough to send the very best," Ian drawled.

Cy shook his head, his expression somber. "If someone's mad or crazed enough to shoot at someone, there are usually signs beforehand. He must have tried to make *some* attempt to connect with Mac, but damned if I can find anything."

Cate listened, hating what she was hearing. She had taken a series of photos of Noah and the others when the meeting had first started, capturing the business that went on behind the creativity of the music scene. Noah, chewing thoughtfully on the end of a pencil as he listened to his manager. Noah, a line of concentration across his brow as he read a contract. Noah first, last, and always . . .

She wandered toward the other end of the room, where Bonnie was doing needlework. Lord, she wished Cy or the police would find out who this madman was and why he was trying to kill Noah.

She lifted her camera, checking the angle from down the length of the room, then got off a couple of shots of him, a distant, remote figure surrounded by staff. It was how most people who didn't know him saw him, she thought. It was how she had seen him until she had come to stay there and realized that in many ways he was still very alone and needy, just as she was.

The people around him shifted, widening the space around him. On impulse she snapped another series of shots that were of him alone, framed with the turquoise glass sculpture of the owl, glowing with light, and against the luster and luxury of a raw silk chocolate-colored columned drape. The shot would show a complex man filled with darkness who surrounded himself with the comforts of his wealth and the whimsy and light that obviously still resided somewhere in his soul.

Just then he raised his head and looked down the room at her. She wasn't close enough to him to see the expression in his eyes, but it didn't matter. Heat sprang full blown in the pit of her stomach. She'd become his lover, sharing a wild and incredibly hot intimacy with him. The time she'd spent with him had been life-changing for her in many ways. She just wished she could have the faith that the outcome would be a happy one. She dropped back down on the couch.

"Did you know that Gloria is back?" Bonnie asked casually.

Cate had been so engrossed in Noah, she'd almost forgotten Bonnie was at the other end of the couch. She made a futile attempt to brush order into her bangs, a habit that was at the moment providing her a much-needed distraction from Noah. "No, I didn't. Where is she?"

"Sleeping off jet lag. She'll probably get up for dinner."

Cate glanced over at Dorsey. He was listening to something Ian was saying, a smile on his face. Who knew what he was really thinking? Did he even care that the beautiful woman who loved him was back?

She turned to Bonnie, watching as she jabbed a needle in and out of needlepoint mesh. "What are you working on?" Shifting, she tried to get a better look at it.

Bonnie held it up, and her fingers outlined the tracings on the mesh. "It's for Juliette. There's going to be a blue elephant here, a pink and white zebra there, and a polka-dot giraffe between them. When I finish, I'll frame it and put it over her crib."

"It's charming," she said sincerely, then changed her tone to one of teasing. "But aren't you afraid she'll grow up confused, looking at that?"

"You mean, am I afraid my child will grow up thinking elephants are actually blue and zebras pink and white?" Serenely Bonnie rubbed her bulging stomach. "We'll take her to the zoo so that she can see the real thing, but we'll also tell her that the world is what you see with your imagination as well as what you see with your eyes."

Cate nodded, thinking that she of all people should understand what Bonnie was saying. She didn't simply capture the surface with her pictures, she also tried to show what was beneath. "Bonnie, if your little girl only knew what a neat mom was waiting for her, she'd come out today."

Bonnie laughed. "Lord, I hope not. We don't have anything ready for her yet."

"She'll have you and Ian. What more could any baby want?"

Bonnie reached over and briefly clasped Cate's hand. "That's a lovely thing to say, and you're a lovely person. I'm so glad to see that you're looking much happier these past couple of days."

"I am?"

Bonnie nodded. "Definitely. In *spite* of the sniper."

If she looked on the outside the way Noah's lovemaking made her feel on the inside, she thought wryly, she was probably glowing. She was trying to decide how to respond, when she heard a burst of laughter from the group. She glanced at them and saw Noah laughing at something Dorsey had said to him. "Bonnie, how does everyone feel about what has happened?"

"You mean the shots that were taken at you and Mac? Awful, of course. We all love Mac and can't stand the idea that somebody's after him."

"What about frightened?"

Bonnie shrugged and went back to her needlepoint. "Of course—that too. I mean, when you think about it, life is pretty frightening, but what's the point of letting fear rule you? Over the years Ian has had obsessed fans. I'm sure there's no one in the public eye who hasn't. But most of them are simply frustrated, lonely people trying to reach out and make contact with someone they admire."

"You seem very relaxed about it."

Humor glinted in Bonnie's eyes. "I guess I can afford to be relaxed about it this time. Ian and I aren't the ones who were shot at."

"But what if you were? What would you do?"

Bonnie laughed. "You mean after Ian called out the National Guard to protect me?"

A smile tugged at her lips. "Yeah, I can see him doing that."

"We're about to become parents for the first time. Now more than ever we can't let a fan, or, for that matter, anyone else dictate how we live, and Mac won't either."

"But he had his staff come here today instead of going to them, and he's told me not to go for any walks."

Bonnie's expression was kind. "Ian's told me the same thing, but it's a temporary alert, that's all. After a few days, if nothing else happens, life will get back to normal. You can't stop life, you know. And as for the staff, they often come out here. They like the beach. In fact, under normal circumstances we'd all have a cookout down there this evening."

Cate studied Bonnie. The young mother-to-be looked so ethereal she sometimes appeared to Cate in need of tethering to the earth to prevent her from floating away. But in Bonnie's case, Cate had learned looks were definitely deceiving. "I have to tell you that I'm absolutely in awe of you."

Bonnie looked surprised. "Me?"

"Yes, you. You live smack in the middle of all this rock-star hoopla, yet you manage to stay serene and centered. And not only that, but you maintain a strong and loving relationship, *and* you're planning a family."

Bonnie's expression was mildly quizzical as she returned Cate's gaze. "But what are my options? Living without Ian? No, Cate. That's unacceptable."

The staff left an hour later, but the band stayed, along with Bonnie. The housekeeper came in with drinks and snacks for everyone. The conversation was light, sprinkled with a lot of in jokes that went right over Cate's head. Some were explained to her, some weren't, but she wasn't offended by those that weren't. In subtle ways she was beginning to feel a degree of acceptance from the others.

She couldn't decide whether it was because of something Noah might have said to them, or whether they sensed what Noah was feeling for her, or simply the fact that she had been in the line of fire with their beloved leader. Whatever the reason, the hostility emanating from them today was definitely less. Whereas before, Ian's, Dorsey's, and Santini's usual pattern was to ignore her, they now included her, though granted it was in a rather offhanded, absentminded fashion. And she found herself beginning to relax and enjoy the banter.

At one point Noah looked at her and patted the cushion beside him. "Come over here, and I'll share some of this great dip."

The invitation was casually given, but Dorsey, Ian, Santini, and Bonnie all turned to look at her. There was no chance they would think he was simply playing the part of the affable host, she reflected—something he obviously knew. No, the invitation might have seemed casual, but it wasn't, and everyone in the room knew it. She couldn't begin to guess why he had decided that now was the time to let his friends in on what was between them; she supposed he had his reasons. And after she thought about it for a moment, she decided there was really no reason not to take him up on his invitation. She rose and went to his side.

He scooped up a portion of the Mexican seven-layer dip on a taco chip and offered it to her. "Cate and I have known each other for quite a while," he said to the others, watching her as she munched the chip. "In fact, we've known each other since we were children."

"How come you haven't told us that until now?" Ian drawled, eyeing Cate with new interest.

Bonnie spoke up. "Ian, they're entitled to their privacy."

Noah held up his hand. "No, it's okay. It's just that Cate and I've never told anyone about our friendship."

"Friendship?" Suspicion laced Dorsey's voice, and he looked directly at Cate as he spoke.

"We've always loved each other," Noah said simply, looking at her. "Always."

His expression was set, warning her not to disagree with what he was saying, and she had no intention of doing so. He was telling the truth, and besides, these people were his friends, and he had every right to make the decision.

At the beginning of the assignment she had enjoyed the relative anonymity of being just a photographer in the eyes of the band, but once things began heating up between her and Noah, some part of her had known the secret of their relationship would be shared with them.

"I think that's wonderful," Bonnie said into the silence. "Really."

Cate sympathized with everyone's plight. They were wondering what kind of love Noah was talking about, and she couldn't blame them. But in her view, that particular subject was still too new and personal to talk about. And apparently Noah agreed, because he proceeded to switch the subject.

As he troweled a chip through the dip, he sent Bonnie a look. "So how's Juliette treating you these days? Is she letting you sleep?"

Bonnie took the cue. "It depends. Some nights I could swear she's going to be a Rockette, the way she kicks, but Ian is convinced she's going to be a soccer player." She smiled at her husband. "In fact, he's already making noise about looking into soccer leagues."

Ian straightened; obviously he was very much taken with the idea. "Sure. In fact, I may coach. We probably won't do much touring in the next few years. That'll give me a chance to get her started and—"

Just then Cy walked in, carrying a rectangular white box, his expression so grim, everyone immediately fell silent. To Cate's eyes, even his usual wildly patterned shirt seemed more subdued than usual.

He crossed to Noah. "You said you wanted to see everything, well, this is the latest. We found it at the foot of the drive, right outside the gate." He put the box in Noah's outstretched hand. "It's safe—I've checked it for wires. But if you want to pick it up, be careful and touch only the fabric."

Frowning, Noah lifted the lid off. Cate leaned toward him and peered in. It was a beautiful doll about eighteen inches high. She had blond hair and was wearing a blue gingham and lace dress, gold beads circling her neck. Her eyes were closed and her thick brown lashes shadowed her cheeks.

Cate's forehead creased with puzzlement as a sense of unease crept over her.

"It's a doll," she murmured, informing the others who couldn't see into the box as well as she could.

Noah looked up at Cy. "A doll? Someone left a *doll* at the gate?"

Cy silently handed him a note. "This came with it."

Noah took it and read aloud. " 'I missed you two days ago, but sooner or later I'm going to get you.' "

Santini recoiled as if he had been hit.

Dorsey uttered a curse.

Ian reached for Bonnie's hand.

A muscle flexed in Noah's jaw. "So this is from our friend on the hill, and it seems he's still very determined."

"But why a doll?" Bonnie asked. "I don't get it."

"I don't either," Noah said, reaching in and lifting the doll out, careful to keep his fingers on the fabric of her skirt.

As he raised the doll, her eyes opened, and Cate's hand flew to her mouth, stifling a gasp.

Where the eyes had once been, there were now only gaping, empty sockets. The doll's eyes had been gouged out

Noah's expression turned dark. "What the hell?"

Santini sat forward, his expression somber. "Whoever this guy is, he's one sick puppy."

Cy uttered a low curse. "I'll telephone the police. They'll want to see this."

"Wait a minute, Cy. I don't suppose anyone saw who left this."

The big man shook his head. "No. We're not even sure exactly when it was left. I'm sorry."

"It's not your fault." Noah glanced at Cate. "Are you all right?"

"Fine," she said faintly, unable to stop staring at the doll. It would have been a doll any little girl would have loved to own—except for the empty eye sockets. They made the doll's beauty frightening and grotesque.

She tried to think, tried to reason out this new occurrence. Someone had taken a knife or a screwdriver and had dug the eyes out. Why? What kind of message was the person trying to send? The person had lain up on the hill and shot at Noah with a high-powered rifle. And then that same person had sent a doll. But the doll was a *girl* doll. Not a boy doll.

Her gaze left the empty eye sockets and dropped to the doll's body. And for the first time she focused on the gold beads around the doll's neck that lay nestled in the ruffled collar. And she went cold.

"Cate, what's wrong?" She felt Noah's hand on her arm. "Cate honey, what is it? You're white as a sheet."

"Someone get her a glass of water," Bonnie said urgently.

Cate slowly lifted her hand and pointed toward the gold beads that circled the doll's neck. "That's my bracelet." Her voice was just a whisper, yet she felt as if she were screaming.

"How can it be . . ." Noah's voice trailed off, then picked back up, stronger than ever. "It *can't* be your bracelet, Cate. It's only a trinket."

"No, it's mine," she said, staring at it. "And it's real amber. I recognize the irregularity of the beads' shape. I bought it in Europe last year."

"Couldn't it be one that *looks* like yours?" Cy asked.

She would have loved to have believed that, but she didn't. "Look on the clasp. If it says eighteen karat, Italy, then it's mine. No manufacturer would put real gold jewelry on a doll."

Cy took the doll from Noah, and using the eraser end of a pencil, carefully tipped the clasp until he could read. " *'Eighteen karat, Italy.'* "

Cate glanced around the room, pausing to focus on each person there, then she looked back at Noah. "You know what this means, don't you? Those bullets yesterday weren't meant for you. They were meant for me."

He slowly shook his head. "No."

He didn't want to believe it, she thought, but she knew in her heart it was true.

"But why would anyone want to kill you?" Bonnie asked incredulously.

"I haven't the faintest idea."

"Do you have any clue about who it could be?" Cy asked.

"Not a one."

She felt so stupid. She should know the answers to these questions. If there was a person out there somewhere who hated her so much that he wanted to kill her, shouldn't she *know*?

She remembered her first instinct yesterday after the bullets had hit. Noah had told her that the person was shooting at him, but it hadn't made sense to her that anyone would want to kill him. Yet he and Cy had seemed so sure . . .

Noah was rubbing her hand, and she heard Bonnie say, "She's in shock."

She drew her hand from Noah's. "No, I'm fine. Really." She saw that they were all looking at her oddly. How could she blame them? Suddenly she felt totally isolated. And very exposed.

She was a target, and she didn't know for what or for whom.

She wondered if Noah had felt the same way yesterday. He certainly hadn't given any sign. He had seemed to accept it as part of his job. His main concern had been to get her away from him, away from the danger, and now she knew exactly how he felt. Because that was what she was going to have to do. She was going to have to leave him so that he could stay safe.

She turned and found him looking at her worriedly.

"If that is your bracelet—"

"It is."

"Okay, do you have any idea how someone could have gotten it?"

She slowly shook her head. "Not really."

"When's the last time you saw it?" Cy asked.

She thought for a minute. "I keep it in my jewelry box on my dresser in my apartment, but since I don't wear any jewelry when I work . . ." Her words drifted off as she remembered the occasional spooky feeling she'd gotten the past few months that someone had been in her apartment. A chill raced down her spine.

With a touch of a finger to the side of her jaw, Noah urged her to look at him. "What, Cate?"

"I don't remember the last time I wore it." She made a vague gesture. "I just assumed it was still in the box, along with the rest of my jewelry. I don't check its contents daily or even monthly." She laughed weakly. "On top of everything else, it appears I've been robbed."

"Cy, get the police out here."

TEN

Noah found Cate in the darkened guest bedroom, curled up small and tight in a chair in the corner. She was so still, it seemed to him she barely breathed. She had withdrawn into herself, he realized, and he felt constitutionally incapable of allowing that condition to go on. He needed her too damned much.

He snapped on a lamp. "What are you doing sitting in here in the dark?"

She blinked her eyes against the light. "I guess I hadn't realized how dark it had gotten. Have the police gone?"

"Yes." He dropped down onto the side of the bed, facing her. She looked pale and drawn. The sight made him want to tear something apart, preferably the person who was causing her so much grief. "They took the doll and note with them for lab analysis, but they weren't too hopeful. These days even the most rank amateur knows to wear gloves. But they can also run it through the computer to see if anything similar has happened to anyone else. A doll with its eyes gouged out is pretty distinctive."

She felt so cold, had for hours now. "No, I suppose not. In fact, on a scale of one to ten, I'd say it rates pretty high on the weird meter, wouldn't you?"

"Yeah, pretty much." His mouth drew into a grim line.

She looked at him. "They're not going to be able to help, are they?"

He leaned forward, rested his elbows on his knees, and clasped his hands together. "It's too early to say for sure. Any guess would be just that, a guess. The problem is that you didn't give them anything to go on."

She made an astonished sound. "Do you think I did that on *purpose*? Noah, I didn't give them anything to go on, because I don't *know* anything."

"Why didn't you tell me you'd been having trouble?"

She sighed. She'd known sooner or later she'd have to answer this question. "Because it was nothing I could put my finger on exactly, only little things really. There were times I thought I had to be mistaken, that I was simply overworking and was too tired and that my imagination was running away with me."

"You never thought about contacting the police?"

"Maybe once or twice, but the things that were happening were too vague. I mean, now and then everyone gets a phone call in the middle of the night or thinks she sees shadows where there shouldn't be any. People are always forgetting where they put things."

"You were trying to put a reasonable face on something that wasn't at all reasonable," he said bleakly. "But at least all of that helped make up your mind to come here."

"I was hoping that by leaving my life, so to speak, and coming here, where I would be fairly isolated, whatever was causing the problem—whether it was me or something else—would simply go away and that by the time I got back my life would be normal again."

With his brow creased in a worried frown, he came down on his knees in front of her and gently brushed her hair back from her pale face. The expression in her eyes was hunted. His mouth tightened at the sight, but he kept his voice soft. "I know this has all been a shock to you. It's bound to have been. But, honey, you must know something. Even if it's something that seems insignificant to you, it still might help shed light on all of this."

She drew her feet up into the chair and wrapped her arms tightly around her legs, physically pulling away from him as far as she could.

"I told the police everything. I can't think of anything else I might know." Suddenly a shudder ran through her. "Lord, Noah, that doll's *eyes*. God, I wish I understood. What on earth could the person who left it have been trying to tell me?"

With a broken sound she dropped her head onto her knees. The sound drilled straight through him. He felt so helpless, and it was the one feeling in the world he couldn't tolerate. He had felt helpless that long-ago stormy night, right before he'd run for the gun. And in the end he still hadn't been able to help his mother. The memory multiplied his determination a thousandfold. He *wouldn't* watch Cate die in front of him as he had had to watch his mother.

He stroked his hand over her bowed head. "I don't know what the person was saying with that doll, but I think we should talk about it, throw out ideas. Between us maybe we can figure something out."

She lifted her head, once again dislodging his hand. "No, this is my problem. You don't have the time to mess with this. You've got the concert to prepare for."

"The concert be damned, Cate. Nothing is more important to me than keeping you safe."

The laugh she gave was filled with sorrow. "Well, then, that's where you're wrong. The concert sold out this morning and all those people are expecting to see you perform. You can't disappoint them. Besides, it's for a great cause."

Impatience created spiked edges in his voice. "Forget the damned concert, Cate. Okay? No one is going to be disappointed. I'll work it out, but right now it's you I'm concerned about."

She gave a long sigh. Then carefully, deliberately, she lowered her feet to the floor. "Listen, Noah, I've been thinking. I need to get back home."

In one smooth, sudden move he stood and dragged a hand through his hair. "I guess I should have anticipated this, but I didn't." His voice was knife sharp now, cutting and slicing its way through the air to her. "No way, Cate. You're not going home."

"The police are going to be checking out my apartment, and I'll need to be there."

"You gave them a key. They can check it out by themselves."

She gazed up at him, determination etched in her features. "I've got to go home, Noah. This person, whoever he is, wants me, not you."

"Oh, I see, and because he wants you, you're going to make it easy for him. That makes perfect sense, Cate. Perfect."

His sarcasm penetrated her skin like needles and

hurt her deep inside. "It makes sense to me. Every person on this estate is in danger as long as I'm here."

"Then I'll send everyone away with the exception of the security."

Her eyes lit briefly with hope. "And you'll go?"

"No, Cate. I'm staying with you."

She gave an angry exclamation. "And by staying you'll put yourself smack in the middle of something that doesn't involve you at all."

"How do you know I'm not involved? Something must have happened to trigger this lunatic. You said yourself that before you came here, only little things had happened. Well, guess what? It seems to me that *I'm* the only thing in your life that has changed."

"But how would he know that?"

"Maybe he doesn't. Maybe he's guessing. Or maybe it's not you and me, but the assignment itself that's got him flipping out."

She shook her head. "That makes no sense. There's nothing threatening to anyone about this photo shoot."

"Who says it has to make sense? Like Santini said, this guy is one sick puppy."

She folded her arms around her waist, fighting off the chill. "I realize now that he's been watching me all along. In fact, he probably knows most everything about me. For sure he knew my schedule. He had to know, because he felt so free to go in and out of my apartment, move things, take the bracelet." No matter how hard she tried, she couldn't control another shudder that racked her body. "God only knows what else he did." Tears threatened. She blinked them away, but she couldn't stop the bile from rising in her throat. "Lord, Noah, someone has been crawling around in my life without my knowing about it."

He wanted nothing more than to take her into his arms, comfort her, and tell her he'd protect her with his life. But in her current mood she wouldn't thank him for such a gesture. Somehow, though, he had to reach her. "Right," he said grimly. "And knowing all that, you're telling me you still want to go back to your apartment. That's pure stupidity, Cate."

She thought quickly. "I could go to a hotel."

He sliced a hand through the air. "You're not going anywhere. There's no way I'm going to let you go from a protected environment to one that's dangerous."

"You've got no choice, Noah." She spoke slowly, quietly, carefully feeling her way through the things she needed to say to him. "I'm not a child anymore who has to cling to you when I get scared. I've lived on my own a long time now. I can manage."

"Oh, sure you can, Cate. Just like you've done

up to now. As you put it, someone's been crawling around in your life, and you didn't even know about it. Think! Do you know how superior this guy must have felt? How much in charge?"

She knew, and the thought made her absolutely sick. "You can't change my mind, Noah."

He stared at her for a moment. Then almost perceptibly the tension eased from his body, and he slipped his hands into his pockets. "You know what? I find this all really interesting."

Cate looked up at him, confused. "Interesting?"

"Yesterday at this time I was trying to get you to go home so that you would be removed from what I then perceived as a dangerous situation. You told me I was being selfish and that you didn't care what I wanted. You flat out refused to go. Well, using the same damned criterion, Cate, who is it who's being selfish now?"

She eyed him dubiously. "Things have changed."

"They sure have, haven't they? The tables have completely turned. This time you're trying to protect me. And you know what else? It's really strange. You wouldn't commit to marrying me, but you're willing to put your life on the line to protect me."

"It's not like that."

"It's *exactly* like that, Cate. I plan to be every bit as stubborn on this as you were yesterday. You're not leaving. You're going to stay right here, where I can protect you. You got that?"

She wasn't going to win the argument, she realized. But in the end, who won this particular argument didn't matter. Ultimately she would do what she had to do.

He held out his hand. "Come on. Let's go to dinner. Everyone's waiting for us."

"You go. I'm not hungry." Her mouth twisted wryly. "Besides, they're waiting for you, not me."

"You're wrong. They're concerned about you, especially Bonnie. Come on. You don't want to upset her, do you?"

Her eyes narrowed. "Blackmail, Noah?"

He grinned. "Anything that will work, Cate." His grin slowly faded. "And after dinner we're going to go to my room and make love for so many hours and so hard, you won't have the strength to go anywhere for a long, long time."

"Maybe it *would* be a good idea if everyone went back home for a while," Noah was saying to the table at large.

Ian scowled. "What about the concert?"

Noah shrugged. "It can go on as planned. It's still a few weeks away, but strictly speaking, we don't really need that much rehearsal for it. We know our old material cold, and the new stuff can wait."

"Or," Cate said, compelled to speak up, hoping to get the band to agree with her and thereby influence Noah, "I can leave and all of you can get on with your lives."

Bonnie's china-blue eyes took on a surprising steel glint. "You don't want to do that. If you left, you would have no protection."

"Exactly," Noah said, not bothering to hide his satisfaction that Bonnie had echoed him so perfectly. "But I am concerned about all of you. That's why it might be best to take a break and go back home until this blows over."

Watching as the three band members exchanged one of their patented only-they-know-what-it-means glances, Cate had to agree with Noah. Even though she still planned to leave, things had happened on the estate that had to be making everyone uneasy. It *would* be better if they all left. "I'd like to apologize to all of you about this disruption in your work. I wish I could fix it, but I can't get a handle on what's happening. Maybe you could resume your studio work in another place."

"There's no need for you to apologize," Santini said. "It's not your fault."

Somewhat astonished by his remark, Cate took a moment to think about it. And then she realized that if anyone in the world would understand what it meant to be stalked by an obsessed stranger, it would be this group of people, sitting at the table tonight—four rock stars, a superstar model, and a woman who loved one of those rock stars.

Looking rested and beautiful in a simple gold sheath and matching sandals, Gloria spoke up. "Dorsey described the doll to me. That must have been an awful moment for you."

She nodded, remembering the horror she had felt at the sight of the doll's eyes. "Yes, it was."

"Have you given any thought to the significance of the doll?"

"I've tried my best, but I haven't come up with a thing. I must have had a doll when I was very young, but I can't remember. At any rate, even if I did, how could it be important?"

"Maybe whether you ever had a doll or not is not what's important."

Something in Gloria's voice alerted Cate to the fact that the model had more on her mind than casual sympathy. Even Dorsey, she noticed, was looking at Gloria curiously. "Then what?"

"I think the gouged-out eyes might be the key."

Noah sat forward. "I agree that's important, but we haven't been able to figure out how or why. Do you have a theory?"

Gloria threw a brief glance at Dorsey from beneath her lashes, then looked back down the table at Cate. "Because of my profession, I'm probably more aware than most of the impact a photograph can have. And your photographs, Cate, have a bigger impact than most." She smiled. "You *see* things with your camera that other people don't."

"I see things," Cate repeated more to herself than to anyone else.

Noah understood. "And whoever this person is, he doesn't want you to see something, Cate. He wants to blind you . . ." He trailed off, unable to to say the words.

"By killing you," Santini finished matter-of-factly.

Cate was stunned. There was someone walking around in her life who saw her photographs as a threat, so much so he wanted to kill her. No matter how hard she tried, she couldn't seem to take the fact in.

"You know," Dorsey drawled into the silence. "I really don't want to go back home. I'm comfortable in the bungalow. We all do pretty good work in the studio here." He spread his hands out. "I'm happy where I am."

Gloria's lovely mouth curved into a smile. "I am too."

Santini's ice-blue gaze swept around the table. "Me too."

Bonnie reached for Ian's hand. "We are too."

Cate couldn't believe her ears. "Are you all crazy? Why would you want to stay here, when you could all go someplace else and be safe?"

Dorsey reached for his wineglass. "We'll be as safe here as we will be anyplace. Besides, we have work to do."

Noah grinned at his friends. "Thanks, guys. I appreciate it."

Santini raised a pasta-ladened fork. "Hey, you can't make music without us."

Ian's laugh boomed out over the room. "Basically because we won't let you."

Bonnie beamed her approval at him, and his usually tough expression melted into one of adoration.

Cate shook her head. "You all realize, don't you, that just because Gloria might have figured out a motive for the guy doesn't mean I know who the person is?"

"Yeah," Noah said, "but now you can start narrowing down the field."

"Narrowing down the field? Do you know how many people look at my photographs in any given month?"

He smiled at her consternation. "See, you've already thought of a way to begin. You can start with the people who subscribe to *Spirit*."

Santini grinned. "And we can all stake out grocery stores and the airports to see who picks up a copy at the newsstands."

Dorsey's eyes glinted behind his glasses. "And then we can cross-check the lists."

Santini raised his hand. "I get to do background checks on all the young, attractive women."

Ian hurled a piece of garlic bread at him. "I've noticed over the years the regrettable lack of young, attractive women in your life."

Santini caught the bread with his left hand. "Yeah, well, let me tell you something, Mr. Happily-Married-About-to-Become-a-Father . . ."

Cate sat back and listened to the banter, remembering her first dinner at this table and the hostility that had been directed her way. Now in their own way they accepted her and were supporting her. True, the reason behind their support and acceptance had more to do with Noah than it did with her, but still their sympathy was very real, and she appreciated it more than she could begin to say.

But now she had to decide what she was going to do.

A decision didn't come easily. Cate was terrified and she was in love, two states of mind and body at opposite ends of life's emotional spectrum, each emotion all-consuming.

Someone wanted her dead. While she could acknowledge that fact intellectually, she couldn't accept it emotionally.

In her entire life she'd never intentionally hurt anyone, but she knew that violence existed. She had lost her biological parents in a violent car crash. Noah had had personal experience with violence at a young age. Some of her best work showed pictures that stripped back surface layers of seeming beauty and showed the violence that teemed beneath. She'd also photographed hate and prejudice. But none of it, not the violence, the hate, or the prejudice, had ever been directed at her.

Fear had moved into her body and taken over, making her doubt and question herself, clashing and conflicting with the new love that was also in her.

She was in love. Totally and completely.

Noah had come into her life early, then had left. And for so many years she'd been alone. But by anyone's standards she'd made a success of her life. She earned good money doing what she loved. She had a host of casual friends, people she could call up for dinner or a movie if she was in the mood. Of course there was no one she'd ever let really close, no one to whom she could bare her soul and heart.

And then, of her own choosing she had walked back into Noah's life. Had she subconsciously hoped they would become lovers? Maybe. Had she subconsciously hoped they would fall in love, *adult* love? She thought not. Even in her wildest, most secret dreams, that had been too much to hope for. Yet it had happened.

Love and terror. She was consumed and torn apart by both.

Noah didn't let her go back to the guest bedroom. In fact, before she could stop him, he personally moved all her things into his room, and then he kept his promise, making love to her every chance he got with such power and intensity she was left exhausted.

He continued rehearsals and laying down new tracks with the band. She continued shooting pictures.

But time, she felt, was running out.

Their lovemaking took on a sense of urgency, and she understood why. They had lost each other before, and they both knew there was a real chance they could lose each other again.

And then, after yet another night of passion, they awoke to new clouds on the horizon and frightening news.

ELEVEN

Giant ferns edged the relatively secluded terrace that extended out from the den's French doors; white roses climbed nearby trellises. Cate sipped her coffee, thankful for the opportunity to have breakfast outside, where she could feel the sea breeze against her skin and smell the brine of the ocean and the scent of the roses. She'd felt stifled and confined these last few days. In short, she'd felt like a victim, and she hated that.

She gazed toward the horizon. The moodiness of the day's atmosphere suited her. Charcoal-colored clouds were building and stacking out over the ocean. Hanging baskets brimming with red geraniums blew back and forth in the breeze, and above them sea gulls flew eastward, inland.

A storm was coming, and it was going to be a bad one.

She glanced across the table at Noah. His head was bent over the morning paper. Only a few strands of his ebony hair remained wet from the shower they had taken together earlier. Even though the width of a table separated them, she thought she could smell the scent of his aftershave. Of course she knew it had to be her imagination, but the truth was, his scent was embedded into her consciousness. "Noah, I was wondering if I could ask for a favor."

He looked up at her with surprise. "A favor? You can have anything you want. Name it."

She smiled. "You'd better be careful. I might ask for the moon."

"No problem—I've got a lasso."

She laughed. "A lasso isn't necessary. I was wondering if you could spare, or if you would have access to, an extra pair of tickets for your concert, some that are for really good seats."

He put his paper down with a frown. "Tickets? You don't need any tickets, Cate. You can have the best seat in the house, by the side of the stage."

Her smile broadened. "And to think, I used to have to save my pennies for a nosebleed seat. And the one time I did get a good seat, well, I won't tell you what I had to go through to get that one."

"I don't want to know, because I'd probably

have to do something dire to you. All you had to do was call me."

"Yeah, right, but barring that . . ." She pointed an accusing finger at him. "You have no idea what people go through to see you and the band perform."

His dark eyes lit with humor. "You sound as if it's my fault."

"I don't know whose fault it is—the system's I guess. At any rate, the tickets aren't for me. They're for a young reporter at the magazine, a coworker of mine, named Marcy. I called my boss yesterday to see what she thought of the pictures I've sent her so far—she was delirious by the way—anyway, Marcy answered the phone and she's desperate for a ticket. I'd like to treat her, if I could. I remember what it was like dying to see you and not having the money for a good seat."

His frown reappeared. "If I'd had any idea—"

"I'm sorry I brought that up. It's the past anyway. We're together now."

He leaned back in his chair. "Of course you can have tickets. You can have as many as you want."

"Thank you. Just two. Marcy will be in heaven."

"Mac!"

Cate turned and saw Cy hurrying across the lawn toward them with one of the men who worked for him following close behind carrying a walkie-talkie that crackled with activity.

She took one look at their somber faces and knew something bad had happened. Careful not to spill any coffee, she set her cup down and folded her hands together.

"What is it?" Noah asked.

"Trouble. We found one of the guards beaten and unconscious about twenty yards inside the front gate. Our security has been breached. You two need to go inside and stay there until we can do a thorough check. Someone could be anywhere on the estate."

Without a word, Noah rose, came around the table, and with a hand on her arm pulled her into the house with him. Cy and the guard followed. The guard immediately went to stand in the doorway that led to the hall and spoke into the walkie-talkie. Cy stayed with them.

Dread was like ice in Cate's veins. "Is the man who was hurt going to be all right?"

Cy's heavy-lidded eyes showed cold determination. "I hope so. There's an ambulance on the way, so are the police, and someone is checking the house right now."

"What about the band?" Noah asked.

"None of them is up yet, but there's a guard on each of their bungalows. Mac, this has gone way beyond dicey. If I'm going to have any kind of control over this, I'm going to have to bring in more guards. I don't know who this guy is or what his background is, but often people who have the least knowledge have the best luck. Now, I don't know for sure if this guy falls into that category, but I do know that so far he's been one lucky son of a bitch."

Noah made an angry, abrupt motion with his hand. "Bring in an army. Do whatever you have to do."

"No, wait," Cate said, unable to stand it anymore. "This is getting ridiculous, and I can't continue staying here, putting everyone else in danger. Your security has been breached and someone has been badly hurt. It's simple. I'll leave, and all your problems will be solved."

Noah's face took on a hard, unyielding cast. "You're staying, and that's that. Cy, get the place secure again and then we'll talk."

With a nod and a glance at his man at the door, Cy left.

Cate clasped her hands together in front of her and stared down at them for a moment. "I've made up my mind, Noah, and I don't want to argue about it."

"Neither do I, but count on it, that's just what we'll do if you think for even a minute that I'm going to let you leave here."

"I may have needed your permission to get in,"

she said, a coolness slipping into her tone, "but I don't need anyone's permission to get out."

He exhaled heavily and rubbed his eyes. "One thing at a time, Cate. For now, let's sit tight until Cy gets back."

"You're trying to avoid the inevitable, which is fine, I guess, if you want to do it that way, but just know one thing. I've made up my mind, and you're not going to be able to change it."

He shook his head as if the action would negate her words. "Can't you understand, Cate? I can't face losing you, not now, when we've found each other again."

"I understand," she said sadly. "But I also understand I have to do what I think is best."

Silence fell between them, becoming more strained as it lengthened.

They heard the sirens of the ambulance and the police as they arrived. At one point Cy returned to let them know that the injured guard was on his way to the hospital, still unconscious, and that the police were helping search the grounds.

The idea that the madman trying to kill her could still be close by kept coming back to her. She was terrified, for herself and for everyone on the estate. And she was getting angrier by the minute.

One by one Santini, Ian, and Dorsey checked in with Noah by phone.

"I bet they're sorry they decided to stay," Cate

murmured when Noah hung up the phone the last time.

"They're in a position to do exactly as they want, and they *wanted* to stay."

When people were in a position to do exactly as they wanted, she thought, and could basically order life to their liking, like the band and Noah, who could blame them if they tended to think of themselves as immune to danger? It took a person more grounded in life's realities to recognize danger and its significance. Like her.

She stared out the door. The dark clouds on the horizon seemed to be increasing, doubling in size, turning blacker. "This has been the damnedest season for weather," she said, whispering to herself. "I don't believe I've ever seen so many storm-filled skies."

Noah didn't comment, nor had she expected him to. The weather was the least of what was bothering both of them. A man had been beaten unconscious because of her. There was a chance he could die. Someone was lurking somewhere, waiting for an opportunity to kill her. And all because of the way she took pictures. She thought back to the blades of grass that had been knotted so patiently and so precisely. This was a determined, compulsive person, and she had to do something to stop him.

Almost an hour had passed before Cy returned,

bringing with him Detective Bob Martin, a heavyset police department veteran who had been assigned to head the case.

"We've had a call from the hospital," Cy said. "Ken has regained consciousness and the prognosis is good."

"Ken?" she asked. "That's the guard's name?" She should know the name of the man who lay in a hospital bed now because of her, she thought numbly.

"Ken Murphy," Cy said.

"Ken Murphy," she repeated, wondering if she'd even seen the man.

"And that's the good news."

"What's the bad news?" Noah's voice was quiet.

Cy motioned for Detective Martin to answer the question. "We found a crude bomb under Miss Gallin's car."

Cate sank into the nearest chair.

Noah bent down to her. "Are you all right?"

A hysterical laugh rose in her throat, but she fought it down. "Fine."

"It's been defused," Detective Martin said, continuing. "And the grounds and house are secure."

"Thank you," Noah said, straightening. "We appreciate your help."

"It's not over yet." The detective looked at Cate. "I understand you think this is all related to your work."

She nodded. "So far it's all we've been able to think of, but I still don't have a clue as to who it could be." She stopped and cleared her throat. "However, I think it's time I did something to find out."

"Don't even start, Cate."

She looked up at Noah and saw the warning in his eyes. "I'm sorry, but I have to. I don't have any other choice."

"Dammit to hell, you have plenty of choices!"

"You're wrong, I don't have a one. I've tried staying here, pulling my head in like a turtle, hiding, hoping that the situation would somehow take care of itself. And look what happened— the violence escalated, and someone has been badly hurt. What's more, if I or any one of the people on this estate had decided to move my car for any reason, we would have been killed."

"She's right, Mac," Cy said. "This guy isn't going to go away. He's deadly serious, and you can bet he's getting more and more frustrated. This is only going to get worse. There's something he doesn't want her to see, and he's not going to stop until he's taken care of her, no matter how many people he has to take out in the process."

Until he's taken care of her. A euphemism, she thought, chilled, for killing her. The fear was almost paralyzing, but she knew all too well that her life was going to depend on her ability to outthink and outmaneuver this man.

Detective Martin frowned thoughtfully. "We couldn't allow you to act on your own, Miss Gallin, but we could come up with a plan where we could work with you and you'd be protected."

Noah erupted, his face hard with anger. "Absolutely not! Not unless you can give me an absolute guarantee that she'd be one hundred percent safe." His dark eyes were fixed on the detective with the intensity of a laser. "Can you do that? Can you guarantee me that she'd come out of it without a scratch on her?"

The detective returned his gaze levelly. "There are no guarantees, Mr. McKane."

Noah turned to her. "You see?"

"The question is," Cate said calmly, "do I do something to draw this guy out under circumstances that are favorable to me, or do I wait for him to choose the time and the place, when I would be least expecting him and everything is stacked in his favor?"

"You do neither and stay here. Circumstances aren't going to get much more favorable than here. I've already told Cy to get more people."

She shook her head. "I'm not willing to let this man make me a prisoner, Noah. I can't, it's as simple as that." She turned to the detective. "What do you have in mind?"

———◆———◆———

"Dammit, what are you doing to us? We've finally got a real chance for happiness and you're going to blow it by putting yourself in danger."

Cate's patience had long since dissolved. She and Noah had argued all afternoon and had covered the same ground over and over. She had heard everything he had to say at least twice. He had to know he couldn't change her mind, but he wouldn't stop trying. "We don't have any chance for happiness," she said, her teeth gritted, "not with that man after me."

"You're not leaving here without me, and that's *that*. I'm going with you."

She shook her head. "You do, and you'll put me in more danger, because the police will have to split their attention between the two of us."

"Then they'll just have to put twice as many men on the case."

"You know as well as I do that they simply don't have the manpower for that. They're doing a great deal now."

"Then Cy and the guys can guard me and the police can guard you."

"Talk about a coordination nightmare! It would be the Keystone Kops revisited."

"Dammit, Cate, be reasonable!"

"I am. You're not. Noah, the plan is all set. I'll

leave first thing in the morning, and the police will be with me all the way. I'll be wired, and they'll follow me in unmarked cars when I drive anywhere. When I'm at work there'll be a plainclothes policeman with me at all times, and also staked out at my apartment. I don't see how the plan could be much better."

"I could be with you, that's how it would be better."

She sighed. "Accept it, Noah. This is for the best."

He didn't accept it, he thought, later that evening, sitting with her at a small table placed in front of a cheerful fire in his bedroom, pretending for her sake to be interested in dinner. He *couldn't* accept it. She was asking him to do nothing while she put herself in danger, and he simply wasn't that strong.

He had tried everything he could think of to get her to change her mind, but she was determined. Once again he had come to a point in his life when he wasn't in control. Once again he hated the feeling. *Helplessness.* There *had* to be something he could do. . . .

Outside, the wind had picked up, and every once in a while he heard faint rumblings of thunder off in the distance. A storm was coming, and he couldn't stop it. All he could do was wait, and pray like he had never prayed before that Cate would be safe.

"I'm glad you had the idea for us to eat alone," she said, gazing at him from across the table. "I know everyone a little better now, but I'd still rather spend the evening alone with you. This evening anyway."

He didn't like the resigned, slightly fatalistic tone he thought he heard in her voice. "We have the rest of our lives in front of us. We'll have many, many dinners alone. So many, you'll get tired of seeing me."

She smiled, as he'd meant her to. "Yeah, right. It could happen. Then again, I doubt it."

"After the concert I'd like us to go away together."

"Where?" After arguing with him all afternoon, she was more than willing to talk about the future. Anything, really, as long as it kept both of their minds off of the next day.

"Anywhere you'd like. What do you think? Europe? Australia?"

She stared at him for a moment. "How about the bed?"

"The bed?"

She pointed to her left. "That bed right over there. *Now*." She stood and held out her hand to him. "Let's go to bed."

He didn't take her hand, he took her, sweeping her into his arms and carrying her to the bed.

His desire for her was always just beneath the surface of his skin, running hot and strong. It required nothing at all to break free—the curve of her lips, a glint in her eye, a soft word, a movement of her body. She made him hard instantly. Needy. She involved every one of his senses, every emotion he possessed. For too long he had contained his love for her, moderated it. He'd put his music above her, above everything. But no more. Containment and moderation were things of the past. He not only couldn't control what he felt for her, he didn't want to.

"Cate—" He wanted to tell her how much she meant to him, but she stopped him by pressing her lips against his.

She didn't want to talk; she wanted only to feel. He understood.

He undressed first her, then himself with hands that trembled. His body was caught in the grip of desperate need that only she could satisfy . . . for a while . . . until the next time when she took him into her body.

On the bed he immediately positioned himself between her thighs. Their silky softness rubbed against the sides of his hips, driving him past sanity. He pushed into her, and as her moist velvet flesh tightly sheathed him, a low, rough groan of satisfaction burst from his chest.

He'd wanted her since the beginning of time, he thought. For forever. And now she was his, and he couldn't, *wouldn't* lose her.

Thunder rumbled closer. He slid his hands beneath her buttocks, pulled her up to him, and thrust fiercely into her, trying time after time to imprint her flesh with his. He wanted to sink into her and never leave her. He wanted to continue through eternity, making love to her. Reason had no place in his thinking. His love and need for her was so great, he couldn't let her go, not ever. . . .

Lightning lit the room, followed shortly by a loud crack, then an enormous boom of thunder. Sweat covered his skin, and his breath came in harsh gasps. She wrapped her legs around his hips and held on to him tightly. He felt the sharp dig of her nails into his back, then she arched and stiffened in ecstasy, calling out his name over and over again.

He pulled back and drove into her, escaping the storm, hurtling after his own release. His loins and brain were on fire. Her contractions milked him sweetly, maddeningly, until his release came in a hard, glorious burst that went on and on, draining him completely.

The storm continued, advancing on them with

giant force, but they were safe, warm, and happy, lying beneath the covers, their arms and legs entwined together.

She kissed him, starting on his face and continuing down his neck to his shoulders and his chest. Her lips soothed and reassured him. He tangled his fingers in her hair and heaved a contented sigh. For now at least, he had everything in the world he wanted. Cate was beside him, connected to him in ways that went beyond the physical.

The storm raged. The wind whipped around the house with a mighty force, thunder shattered overhead, shaking the windowpanes; lightning stabbed its electrical brilliance through the darkness.

Noah held Cate tight. She had her mouth close to his ear, murmuring. He wasn't exactly sure what she was saying, but he loved the sound of her soft voice. The storm be damned. He had Cate.

And then the power went off.

All was still and quiet in the house. The only sound in the room was the faint crackling of a now-dying fire. But outside, the storm continued, sounding as if it were tearing the sky and world apart.

"I'd better go check out the power situation."

Cate heard the reluctance in Noah's voice. "No, stay here with me." She cuddled closer to him, savoring the heat of his body, inhaling his musky after-sex scent, and had the satisfaction of feeling his arm tighten around her. "There's nothing you can do about it. The power company will get it back on sooner or later."

"Yeah, but Cy ordered a backup generator a few days ago. I wonder if it's gotten here?"

"Why did he order it?"

He shrugged, picking up a strand of her hair and winding it around his finger. He might not be able to see her very well, but he could certainly feel her, and tactile contact was every bit as erotic as sight. "We weren't sure we'd ever have to use it, but when we had to tighten the security, we thought it best. These storms have bedeviled us. Southern California is not exactly known for storms, which was one of the reasons I opted for a house here." The last was said in a humor-tinged tone.

"Stay with me," she repeated. "Who cares if it's dark?"

"You know something?" His voice took on a huskiness that sent a thrill up her spine. "You've got a point."

He rolled over to his side and slid his hand down her smooth back to the firm roundness of her buttocks. Applying pressure, he pulled her against his rapidly hardening groin. "You have the most amazing effect on me," he murmured, biting at her earlobe.

A warm shudder raced through her. She giggled and heard herself with some surprise. It had been a long time since she had giggled. She smoothed her hand down his chest to his hard abdomen, and then journeyed lower. "I *love* the effect I have on you."

Thunder boomed overhead, then almost immediately there was a boom at the bedroom door. They both jumped.

"*Noah!* It's *Cy!*" Once again his heavy fist connected with the door. "Are you all right?"

With a muffled laugh Cate slid down in the bed and pulled the covers over her head.

"Come on in," Noah called, and heard a tiny squeal from beneath the covers. With a big smile he reached over and patted her head.

Cy entered and swept the beam of his flashlight around the room until he discovered Noah, sitting up in bed, the covers drawn to his waist. "Power's out."

"No kidding," Noah said dryly, and was rewarded with another giggle from beneath the covers.

Cy frowned. "The generator got here, but it hasn't been installed yet. I've got someone calling about the power. Shouldn't be too long." He paused. "Do you need anything?"

"No, *we're* fine." He deliberately emphasized the *we*. "In fact, Cate and I will probably just go back to sleep." He could tell by the expression on Cy's face that he got the message.

"Right. Okay. Sorry I disturbed you. See you in the morning. Call if you need anything."

As soon as Cate heard the door shut, she emerged from beneath the covers. "Bless his heart."

"Bless his heart?" Noah leaned over her to pull open the drawer of the bedside table and rummage through it.

"Bless his heart, he was embarrassed," she said, clarifying. "What *are* you doing?"

"Looking for matches—here they are. And trust me, Cy was not embarrassed. He's seen and done too much to even remember the emotion." He struck a match and lit a tall ivory candle. The wick caught and the flame illuminated the contents of the table, a clock, a lamp, and one of her cameras. He straightened and lay back down, his head on the pillow beside hers.

"So what you're saying is that he's seen you in bed with various women too many times to be embarrassed." Her tone was both wry and rueful.

"Excuse me, but I did *not* say that."

"But that's what you meant."

"No, it is not." Grinning, he picked up her hand and threaded his fingers through hers. "In fact, Cy has never seen me in bed with a woman."

"You expect me to believe that?" Her words were delivered in a teasing lilt, belying the fact that she desperately wanted to believe him.

"Hey," he said softly, turning to her, his expression suddenly serious. "There've been other women, but there haven't been a lot. And I've never loved anyone but you. *Ever*. Okay?"

She nodded, her throat thick with emotion. "Okay. I'm sorry. I guess for one tiny moment I allowed myself to get insecure."

"I want you to be the most secure person in the world. You deserve to be."

"Yeah."

The storm was rumbling in the distance, having passed, and she spoke so softly, he had to lean very close to catch the words.

He tilted her face up to him with a finger beneath her chin. "Don't think about tomorrow. Not yet. You may be leaving in the morning, but right now you're with me."

She smiled, her heart swelling with love. "That I am. In the dark. And we're all alone. So what do you want to do?"

"What do you think?" he asked, his voice a deep growl. He pressed a kiss to her lips. "What do I want to do every time I look at you?"

She wrapped her arms around his neck. "I hope it's the same thing I want to do every time I look at you."

TWELVE

The storm was coming back, Cate thought drowsily, lying on the bed, snuggled in Noah's thick terrycloth robe. In the last few minutes the flashes of lightning had been growing more frequent and the time lapses between the booms of thunder shorter.

She smiled into the darkness. Thankfully the storm didn't seem to be bothering Noah. Maybe because she'd kept him too busy. Her smile broadened, as she remembered. They'd made love once again, and now he was off foraging in the kitchen for food in spite of the fact that the power still wasn't back on yet.

The smile stayed on her face. Not that she was all that hungry, she reflected. She had never felt so completely sated in her life. She wished that this night would never have to end.

But, if there was one thing she was sure of, it was that tomorrow would come. She would help the police find this person who had become so fixated on her, then put the terror behind her. The future was waiting for her and Noah, and she was eager to get started on it.

A dark form appeared in the doorway, drawing her gaze. "What'd you find? Anything good?"

The dark form remained still and quiet.

"Noah?"

The dark form didn't speak.

Ice-cold fear slid down her spine even as her mind tried to grapple with what she was seeing. "Noah?" she whispered.

The dark form moved, coming toward her. Instinctively she scrambled off the bed and onto her feet. Lightning scored the darkness. And she saw the face.

"Gary?" Shocked and bewildered, she stared at Susan's assistant.

Something was very badly out of kilter. Gary was someone she worked with but barely knew. But she understood, without really understanding how she did, that he had come to kill her.

He stopped a foot shy of the end of the bed. "Hello, Catherine. You really didn't know, did you?"

"Know what?" She took a step back.

"That I'm the one who's been trying to kill you."

She could see him more clearly now. She could see that he held a knife in one hand and a gun in the other. She backed up again and bumped into the nightstand.

"Why?"

Only the length of the bed and a couple of feet separated them. The candle's glow showed him dimly, enough so that she could make out the unnatural smile on his face.

"You see everything with that camera of yours. You're all-knowing. You see through pretense. All you have to do is look at a person through the lens and you can see all their dirty little secrets. But you couldn't see me."

Lightning flashed again. He laughed, a high-pitched, aberrant sound that sent terror straight through her. But her mind was working now. Noah would probably be gone awhile. He might even decide to scramble some eggs or take it into his head to check in with Cy. She couldn't depend on him to come and save her, and after a moment's thought she decided she didn't want him anywhere near Gary. "I don't know what you're talking about, Gary."

"You never knew I was watching you. You never knew I was in your apartment, that I touched your things, that I was making myself part of your life.

You could see everything, but you couldn't see me. I made myself invisible to you. It's the way I balanced the scales . . . with your ability to see, I mean."

She slowly reached behind her to the table, feeling for something she could use as a weapon. But there was the candlestick and a lamp. "If you can do all that, then why do you want to kill me?"

His voice changed, became peevish and irritated. "It was that damned assignment."

The lamp was plugged into the wall. If she pulled it hard enough, could she wrench it free before he made his move? "What assignment?"

"You know very well what assignment," he sputtered accusingly. "The anniversary assignment. Susan wanted you to photograph me. If I'd let that happen, everyone would see."

Her fingers brushed against her camera. "See what?"

"You know. You'd already seen that much at least, hadn't you? You'd seen what a bad person I was. And when you took your pictures, everyone would see."

"See that you're bad?" Her hand closed around the camera.

"Of course I'm bad," he snapped irritably. "I've always been bad. Didn't my mother tell me that all my life? She always said it. Always. I heard it morning, noon, and night. So one day last year I decided to be really bad." His smile broadened but remained frighteningly empty. "I buried her out in back of my house in the Valley. I buried her in the garden, planted radishes over her, and told the neighbors I had to put her in a nursing home. No one wanted to go visit her. She was a mean old hag."

She nearly dropped the camera. "Radishes?"

"Big. They grew big . . . and fast, I should have realized before that Mother would make good fertilizer. You know, I've always admired your work. It's all wonderful. But you can understand, can't you, that I couldn't allow you to show the world what I'd done?"

"I can see that, Gary." What was she going to do?

Humming beneath his breath, Noah entered the den, carrying a tray laden with an assortment of goodies he'd found in the refrigerator, including champagne, strawberries, cheese, and chocolate.

A new melody had come into his head sometime during the past few hours. He couldn't wait to pick up his guitar and bring it to life, but his music could wait. Cate came first.

The occasional lightning bolt brightened the

otherwise dark room, and he couldn't stop himself from flinching. That long-ago storm and the events of that night would always be with him. But thank heaven fate had decided to give Cate to him, not just once, when he'd been a moody, desperately hurt, and unhappy boy, but as a man who hadn't let himself admit how badly he'd needed her until she had walked back into his life.

The storm might be outside, but Cate was waiting for him.

He felt better about everything now, including tomorrow. He'd go with Cate. Somehow he would convince her. He simply couldn't *not* go with her. She was everything to him, and he intended to make certain she would stay safe.

The French door. It was ajar.

He stopped and stared at it. He could barely make it out through the darkness, but he could feel the cool damp air against his skin. Hear the rain louder, clearer.

Carefully, he set down the tray.

"You're very clever, Gary." She knew she was only delaying the inevitable by trying to keep him talking. Sooner or later he was going to come at her. He had a knife and a gun and she was armed with only a camera. There was going to be nothing fair about this fight, but fight she would. With her final breath. For her future with Noah.

Thunder cracked overhead. Taking advantage of the noise, she used her finger to slide open the camera's shutter and flick the switch to warm up the flash.

"I know I'm clever."

"How did you get in?"

"I was watching the house when the power went out. I've been watching it for a few days now. Officially I'm on vacation in Mexico. Have you called the office and wondered where I was?"

"Yes." It wasn't the truth. She'd just assumed that he'd been away from his desk and Marcy had been in the area and answered for him.

"Liar," he said composedly. "You didn't wonder. You and I are connected because you're the only one who can see what I really am." He laughed. "You knew, didn't you? You knew it was me that morning I shot at you. I saw the camera on the patio table through the scope. You see things with that camera. That's why I have to kill you. You understand, don't you? *Don't you?*"

"You said you were watching the house, Gary?" She had to keep him as calm as possible until she figured out exactly what she was going to do. When he made his move, she was going to need every edge she could get. She had to figure out how to raise the camera without revealing to him by the light of the candle's glow what she was doing.

"Every night. Since I've been on vacation, I've watched during the day too. They haven't been guarding anything but the grounds around the house. I saw the power go off. I knew that meant the security system would be out. I got in through the doors off the terrace. It was easy, but I didn't know where you'd be. I figured I'd have to explore the house a bit, maybe kill a few people along the way." The casual way he said it chilled Cate to the bone. "Then I had some luck. I heard McKane call you Cate and tell you he was going to the kitchen." He raised the knife to his eye level and idly looked at it. "I didn't know you two were lovers. I bet no one at the magazine knows either, do they?"

Cate was about to lift the camera, when she saw Noah slip into the room behind Gary. Her heart thudded against her rib cage and her mouth went dry.

"Do they, Catherine?"

"No—no, they don't, Gary. You're the only one who knows."

"Too bad I can't tell them. I would have liked to have told them. I expect he'll be back anytime now, and I'll have to kill him too, but really, when you get right down to it, who cares? He's such a bastard anyway, refusing me all those times I sent those letters to him, asking for an interview. I am sorry I'm going to have to kill you though. I told you that, didn't I? I hope you understand."

"I do, Gary." Behind him she saw Noah lift the fireplace poker from the hearth.

"Good, because I need to kill you now, before McKane gets back. Sorry."

He lunged. She stepped to one side, and at the same time lifted the camera and pressed down the shutter button.

At the sound of the shutter he froze, the arm that held the knife raised to shield his face. *"You bitch! Don't take my picture!"*

Noah brought the fireplace poker down on the man's arm. Gary yelled and the knife slipped from his fingers, falling soundlessly to the thick carpet. Whirling, he brought the gun up, but Noah was already bringing the poker back down, this time smashing into Gary's hand. The gun went flying, and Gary crumpled over, crying out in pain.

Six Months Later

Noah emerged onto the stone terrace of the lovely house he and Cate had been staying in for the last three weeks. The house was situated above a secluded white sand beach on the island of Mustique. It was Dorsey's house, and he had lent it to Cate and Noah for their honeymoon.

Cate was on the beach below, lying at the turquoise water's edge on a wide blanket piled with pillows. She looked beautiful in a white cotton skirt and halter top, with her honey-colored hair shining and her skin turned golden by the sun. Just as he was about to join her, she rose, and with a wave started up to him.

He couldn't take his eyes off her as she came up the steps, past brimming pots of hibiscus and thick clumps of fragrant plantain lilies and, farther along, a koi-filled pool. The breeze flirted with the hem of her skirt, and the smile on her face took his breath away.

The last six months had been wonderful, basically because they had been together. Gary Winthrop had been put away, where he would never again be able to hurt anyone. The benefit concert had been a huge success, both critically and financially. All tensions were gone.

She topped the last step and crossed to his side, relaxed and lovely.

"You should have stayed down there. I was about to join you," he said, smiling. "Then again, maybe it's just as well. I've been down there so much, I'm in danger of becoming a beach bum for the rest of my life."

She laughed. "That'll be the day. You've had one guitar or another in your hands every day since we've been here. Where are they all coming from?"

"Dorsey. They're his." He shrugged. "And a few of them are mine."

"Uh-huh." She grinned. "And how many guitars do you have?"

"I'm not exactly sure. I buy them here and there."

"And apparently keep them here and there," she said, a lovely teasing lit in her voice. "But I'm glad, because I can't imagine a world without your music in it."

"You've always been my music, Cate. Always."

She reached out a hand and tenderly caressed his face. "I suppose there *are* advantages to marrying a musician."

"Oh, yeah?"

"Yeah. Some." She grinned again. "For instance, we had terrific music at our wedding. Some of the most famous and best musicians in the world were there and played at the reception."

He took her hand, an expression of mock seriousness on his face. "Yeah, but who played the best music?"

"You did," she said dutifully, her lips twitching. "And of course Ian, Santini, and Dorsey."

"Our wedding was perfect, wasn't it? And the guys made great best men, didn't they?"

She smiled. "Yes, they did. All *three* of them." When Noah first told her that he wanted Santini, Ian, and Dorsey as best men, she hadn't blinked an eye. And on impulse she had asked Gloria and Bonnie to stand up with her. They had both been beautiful in silk and chiffon. Juliette had been there too, precious in soft lace, held securely in her daddy's arms. It had all seemed so right, so perfect.

"Do you think Dorsey will ever ask Gloria to marry him?"

"I don't know. I hope so. She makes him happy, but he can't seem to bring himself to admit that he needs her." He lifted her hand to his lips and kissed its back. "Luckily there's always been a part of me that knew I needed you."

"Luckily," she agreed solemnly.

He pointed toward the horizon. "Looks like an afternoon squall is blowing in."

She gazed up at him, her green eyes clear and bright. "It's not going to be a storm-free life, Noah."

"I know. He brushed the silky strands of her bangs off her forehead, then circled her waist with his arm and drew her against him. "But we're together."

"We're together."

And that said it all, he reflected, holding her close to him. The breeze blew Cate's skirt against her legs as they stood on the terrace, watching the beauty and the power of the storm come toward them across the turquoise sea. It was the way he would always watch storms, with Cate by his side.

THE EDITOR'S CORNER

Discover heavenly delights and wicked pleasures with **ANGELS AND OUTLAWS**! In the six terrific books in next month's lineup, you'll thrill to heroes who are saints and sinners, saviors and seducers. Each one of them is the answer to a woman's prayer . . . and the fulfillment of dangerous desire. Give in to the sweet temptation of **ANGELS AND OUTLAWS**—you'll have a devil of a good time!

Sandra Chastain starts things off in a big way with **GABRIEL'S OUTLAW**, LOVESWEPT #672. When he's assigned to ride shotgun and protect a pouch of gold en route to the capitol building during Georgia's Gold Rush Days, Gabriel St. Clair tries to get out of it! He'd be sharing the trip, and *very* close quarters, with Jessie James, the spitfire saloon singer whose family has been feuding with his for years . . . and whose smoky kisses had burned him long ago. Gabe had been her first love, but Jessie lost more than her heart when Gabe left the mountain. Seeing him again awakens wicked longings, and Jessie responds with abandon to the man who has always known how to drive her wild. Sandra combines humor and passion to make **GABRIEL'S OUTLAW** a sure winner.

In **MORE THAN A MISTRESS**, LOVESWEPT #673, Leanne Banks tells the irresistible story of another member of the fascinating Pendleton family. You may remember Carly Pendleton from **THE FAIREST OF THEM ALL**, and Garth Pendleton from **DANCE WITH THE DEVIL**. This time we meet Daniel, a man who is tired of being the dependable big brother, the upstanding citizen, and only wants the woman who has haunted his dreams with visions of passion that he's never known. Determined to hide her slightly shady past, Sara Kingston resists Daniel's invitations, but his gaze warms her everywhere he looks. Fascinated by the recklessness beneath his good-guy smile, she yields to temptation—and finds herself possessed. Look forward to seeing more stories about the Pendleton brothers from Leanne in the future.

Marcia Evanick delivers her own unique outlaw in **MY SPECIAL ANGEL**, LOVESWEPT #674. Owen Prescott thinks he's dreaming as he admires the breathtaking beauty on the huge black horse who arrives just in time to save his neck! Nadia Kandratavich is no fantasy, but a sultry enchantress who brought her entire family of Gypsies to live on her ranch. Nadia knows she has no business yearning for the town's golden boy, but his kisses make her hot, wild, and hungry. When prophecy hints that loving this handsome stranger might cost her what she treasures most, Nadia tries to send him away. Can he make her understand that her secrets don't matter, that a future with his Gypsy princess is all he'll ever want? Shimmering with heartfelt emotion, **MY SPECIAL ANGEL** is Marcia at her finest.

BLACK SATIN, LOVESWEPT #675 is from one of our newest stars, Donna Kauffman. A dark bar might be the right place for Kira Douglass to hire an outlaw, but Cole Sinclair isn't looking for a job—and figures the lady with the diamond eyes needs a lesson in playing with danger. He never thought he'd be anyone's hero, but somehow she breathes life back into his embittered soul. She's offered him anything to recover her stolen dolphin; now she vows to fight his demons, to prove to him that she loves him, scars and all, and always will. Donna works her special magic in this highly sensual romance.

Our next outlaw comes from the talented Ruth Owen in **THE LAST AMERICAN HERO**, LOVESWEPT #676. Luke Tyrell knows trouble when he sees it, but when Sarah Gallagher begs the rugged loner to take the job on her ranch, something stirs inside him and makes him accept. His gaze makes her feel naked, exposed, and shamelessly alive for the first time in her life, but can she ignite the flames she sees burning in this sexy renegade's eyes? Branding her body with his lips, Luke confesses his hunger—but hides his fear. Now Sarah has to show him that the only home she wants is in his arms. Fast-rising star Ruth Owen will warm your heart with this touching love story.

Rounding out this month's lineup is **BODY AND SOUL**, LOVESWEPT #677 by Linda Warren. Though Zeke North acts as if the smoky nightclub is the last place on earth he wants to be, he's really imagining how it would feel to make love to a woman whose hands create such sensual pleasure! Chelsea Connors is a seductive angel whose piano playing could drive a man mad with yearning, but he doesn't want to involve her in his brother's trouble. Her spirit is eager for the music she and Zeke can make together. Chelsea aches to share his fight and to soothe old sorrows. He's never taken anything from anyone before for fear of losing his soul, but Chelsea is determined to hold him by giving a love so deep he'd have no choice but to take it. Linda delivers a sexy romance that burns white-hot with desire.

Happy reading!

With warmest wishes,

Nita Taublib

Nita Taublib
Associate Publisher

P.S. Don't miss the spectacular women's novels coming from Bantam in March: **SILK AND STONE** is the spellbinding, unforgettably romantic new novel from nationally bestselling author Deborah Smith; **LADY DANGEROUS** by highly acclaimed Suzanne Robinson pits two powerful characters against each other for a compelling, wonderfully entertaining romance set in Victorian England; and finally, **SINS OF INNOCENCE** by Jean Stone is a poignant novel of four women with only one thing in common: each gave her baby to a stranger. We'll be giving you a sneak peek at these terrific books in next month's LOVESWEPTs. And immediately following this page, look for a preview of the spectacular women's fiction books from Bantam *available now*!

Don't miss these exciting books by your favorite Bantam authors

On sale in January:

THE BELOVED SCOUNDREL
by Iris Johansen

VIXEN
by Jane Feather

ONE FINE DAY
by Theresa Weir

Nationally bestselling author of
THE MAGNIFICENT ROGUE
and
THE TIGER PRINCE

Winner of *Romantic Times*
"Career Achievement" award

Iris
Johansen

THE BELOVED
SCOUNDREL

Marianna Sanders realized she could not trust this dark and savagely seductive stranger who had come to spirit her away across the sea. She possessed a secret that could topple an empire, a secret that Jordan Draken was determined to wrest from her. In the eyes of the world the arrogant Duke of Cambaron was her guardian, but they both knew she was to be a prisoner in his sinister plot—and a slave to his exquisite pleasure . . .

"Take off your cloak," he repeated softly as his fingers undid the button at her throat. She shivered as his thumb brushed the sensitive cord of her neck.

"It's not a barrier that can't be overcome." He slid the cloak off her shoulders and threw it on the wing chair by the fire. His gaze moved over the riding habit that was as loose and childlike as the rest of the clothes in her wardrobe. "And neither is that detestable garment. It's merely annoying."

"I intend to be as annoying as possible until you give Alex back to me." She added in exasperation, "This is all nonsense. I don't know what you hope to gain by bringing me here."

"I hope to persuade you to be sensible."

"What you deem sensible. You haven't been able to accomplish that in the last three years."

"Because Gregor took pity on you, and I found his pity a dreadful contagious disease." He stepped forward and untied the ribbon that bound one of her braids. "But I'm over it now. Patience and the milk of human kindness are obviously of no avail. I can't do any worse than I—Stand still. I've always hated these braids." He untied the other braid. "That's better." His fingers combed through her hair. "Much better. I don't want to see it braided again while we're here."

The act was blatantly intimate, and her loosened hair felt heavy and sensual as it lay against her back. He was not touching her with anything but his hands in her hair, but she could feel the heat of his body and smell the familiar scent of leather and clean linen that always clung to him. With every breath she drew she had the odd sensation that he was entering her, pervading her. She hurriedly took a step back and asked, "Where am I to sleep?"

He smiled. "Wherever you wish to sleep." A burgundy-rich sensuality colored his voice.

"Then I wish to sleep in Dorothy's house in Dorchester."

He shook his head. "Not possible." He indicated the staircase. "There are four bedchambers. Choose which one you like. I usually occupy the one at the end of the hall."

She stared at him uncertainly.

"Did you think I was going to force you? I'm sorry to rob you of your first battle, but I have no taste for rape. I'm only furnishing a setting where we'll be close, very close. I'll let Fate and Nature do the rest." He nodded to a door leading off the parlor. "Your workroom. I've furnished it with tools and glass and paint."

"So that I can make you a Window to Heaven?" She smiled scornfully. "What are you going to do? Stand over me with a whip?"

"Whips aren't the thing either. I wanted you to have something to amuse you. I knew you were accustomed to working, and I thought it would please you."

She crossed the parlor and threw open the door to reveal a low-ceilinged room with exposed oak beams. She assumed the dark green velvet drapes covered a window. The room was not at all like her workroom in the tower.

But a long table occupied the center of the room and on that table were glass and tools and paints.

Relief soared through her, alleviating a little of the tension that had plagued her since they had left Cambaron.

Salvation. She could work.

"And you, in turn, will amuse me." He gestured to the large, thronelike high-backed chair in the far corner. "I know you were reluctant three years ago to let me watch you at your craft, but circumstances have changed."

"Nothing has changed." She strode over to the

window and jerked back the curtains to let light pour into the room, then went to the table and examined the tools. "I'll ignore you now, as I would have then."

"You wouldn't have ignored me," he said softly. "If I hadn't been a soft fool, you would have been in my bed before a week had passed. Perhaps that very night."

She whirled on him. "No!"

"Yes."

"You would have forced me?"

"No force would have been necessary."

Heat flooded her cheeks. "I'm not Lady Carlisle or that—I'm not like them."

"No, you're not like them. You're far more alive, and that's where both temptation and pleasure lie. From the beginning you've known what's been between us as well as I have." He looked into her eyes. "You want me as much as I want you."

In the bestselling tradition of Amanda
Quick, a spectacular new historical
romance from the award-winning

Jane Feather

VIXEN

*Chloe Gresham wasn't expecting a warm welcome—
after all her new guardian was a total stranger. But
when Sir Hugo Lattimer strode into Denholm Manor
after a night of carousing and discovered he'd been
saddled with an irrepressible and beautiful young ward,
the handsome bachelor made it perfectly clear he wanted
nothing to do with her. Chloe, however, had ideas of her
own. . . .*

"Come on, lass." Hugo beckoned. "It's bath
time."

Chloe stood her ground, holding on to the back
of the chair, regarding Hugo with the deepest suspicion. "I don't want a bath."

"Oh, you're mistaken, lass. You want a bath
most urgently." He walked toward her with soft-
paced purpose and she backed away.

"What are you going to *do?*"

"Put you under the pump," he said readily,
sweeping her easily into his arms.

"But it's freezing!" Chloe squealed.

"It's a warm night," he observed in reassuring

accents that Chloe didn't find in the least reassuring.

"Put me down. I want to go to bed, Hugo!"

"So you shall . . . so you shall. All in good time." He carried her out to the courtyard. "In fact, we'll *both* go to bed very soon."

Chloe stopped wriggling at that. Despite fatigue and the events of the night, she realized she was far from uninterested in what such a statement might promise.

"Why can't we heat some water and have a proper bath," she suggested carefully.

"It would take too long." He set her down beside the pump, maintaining a hold on her arm. "And it would not convince you of the consequences of headstrong, willful behavior. If you dash into the midst of an inferno, you're going to come out like a chimney sweep." Releasing her arm, he pulled the nightgown over her head so she stood naked in the moonlight.

"And chimney sweeps go under the pump," he declared, working the handle.

A jet of cold water hit her body and Chloe howled. He tossed the soap toward her. "Scrub!"

Chloe thought about dashing out of the freezing jet and into the house, but the filth pouring off her body under the vigorous application of the pump convinced her that she had no choice but to endure this punitive bath. She danced furiously for a few moments, trying to warm herself, then bent to pick up the soap and began to scrub in earnest.

Hugo watched her with amusement and rapidly rising desire. The gyrations of her slender body, silvered in the moonlight, would test the oaths of a monk. She was in such a frantic hurry to get the job over and done with that her movements were devoid of either artifice or invitation, which he found even more arousing.

"I hate you!" she yelled, hurling the soap to the ground. "Stop pumping; I'm clean!"

He released the handle, still laughing. "Such an entrancing spectacle, lass."

"I hate you," she repeated through chattering teeth, bending her head as she wrung the water out of the soaked strands.

"No, you don't." He flung the thick towel around her shoulders. "Rarely have I been treated to such an enticing performance." He began to dry her with rough vigor, rubbing life and warmth into her cold, clean skin.

"I didn't mean to be enticing," she grumbled somewhat halfheartedly, since the compliment was pleasing.

"No, that was part of the appeal," he agreed, turning his attentions to the more intimate parts of her anatomy. "But I trust that in the future you'll think twice before you fling yourself into whatever danger presents itself, my headstrong ward."

Chloe knew perfectly well that given the set of circumstances, she would do the same thing, but it seemed hardly politic or necessary to belabor the issue, particularly when he was doing what he was doing. Warmth was seeping through her in little ripples, and, while her skin was still cold, her heated blood flowed swiftly.

Finally, Hugo dropped the towel and wrapped her in the velvet robe. "Run inside now and pour yourself another tot of rum. You can dry your hair at the range. I'm going to clean myself up."

"Oh?" Chloe raised an eyebrow. "I'm sure it would be easier for you if I worked the pump." She turned up her blistered palms. "I've had a good deal of practice already . . . and besides, I'm entitled to my revenge . . . or do I mean *my* pleasure."

Hugo smiled and stripped off his clothes. "Do your worst, then, lass." He faced her, his body fully aroused, his eyes gleaming with challenge and promise.

With a gleeful chuckle she sent a jet of water over him, careful to circumvent that part of his body that most interested her. Hugo was unperturbed by the cold, having enjoyed many baths under the deck pump of one of His Majesty's ships of the line. The secret was to know it was coming.

With the utmost seriousness he washed himself as she continued to work the handle, but deliberately he offered himself to her wide-eyed gaze. She worked the pump with breathless enthusiasm, her tongue peeping from between her lips, her eyes sparkling with anticipation.

"Enough!" Finally, he held up his hands, demanding surcease. "The show's over. Pass me the towel."

Chloe grinned and continued to work the handle for a few more minutes. Hugo leapt out of the stream and grabbed the damp towel. "You're asking for more trouble, young Chloe." He rubbed his hair and abraded his skin.

"Inside with you, unless you want to go under again." He took a menacing step toward her and with a mock scream she ran into the house, but instead of going to the kitchen she went into Hugo's bedroom, diving beneath the sheets.

When he came in five minutes later, she was lying in his bed, the sheet pulled demurely up to her chin, her cornflower eyes filled with the rich sensuality that never failed to overwhelm him.

"Good morning, Sir Hugo." She kicked off the cover, offering her body, naked, translucent in the pearly dawn light.

"Good morning, my ward." He dropped the towel from his loins and came down on the bed beside her.

> "A fresh and electrifying voice
> in romantic fiction."
> —*Romantic Times*

ONE FINE DAY

Theresa Weir

The bestselling author of *Last Summer* and *Forever* offers her most poignant and passionate novel yet.

After too many years of heartache, Molly Bennet had packed her bags and run away . . . from her memories, her husband, and the woman she had become. But just as she found herself on the brink of a brand-new life, an unexpected tragedy called her home. Now the man who had always been so much stronger than Molly needs her in a way she'd never thought possible. . . .

"If I touch you . . . you won't run, will you? Please . . . don't run away."

And there it was again. That ragged catch in his voice.

And there it was again. Her weakening resolve. Things were so much easier when you knew who the enemy was. "No," she whispered. "I won't run."

He reached for her. His fingers touched her arm, skimming across her skin until he grasped her hand. He pulled her toward him. She took one hesitant step, then another.

He lifted her hand . . . and he kissed it. He kissed the chewed nails that were her shame, that she thought so unsightly. His lips touched her palm, her knuckles. Then he pulled in a shaky breath and pressed her hand to the side of his face. She could feel his beard stubble. She could feel the heat of his skin.

And even though she tried to harden herself against him, it did no good. There was no anger left in her. Instead, what she felt was a sweet, unbearable sadness. A sadness that was much worse than anger.

And she found herself wanting to comfort him. She had to fight the urge to wrap her arms around him and pull his head to her breast.

Austin had never stirred such ineffable emotions in her. All her life she'd taken care of the people around her. Sammy . . . Amy . . . But Austin had always been so strong, so invincible. He'd never needed anybody. He'd certainly never needed her.

The limb above their heads creaked. Crickets sang from the deep grass near the edge of the yard.

Austin took both of her hands in his. "Remember that time, shortly after we first met?" he asked. "It was dark. I took you to the park . . . and pushed you in the swing. Do you remember?"

At first she didn't, but then she did. "Yes."

They had laughed together that night. But since then their marriage had contained very little laughter. What had happened to them? she wondered. Where had that kind of joy gone? Why had two such ill-suited people ever gotten married in the first place?

Had there ever been any kind of love between them? Had there ever been a time when their marriage hadn't been so bad?

If nothing else, she had to acknowledge the fact that Austin had given her what Jay couldn't—security.

She could also admit that there had been a brief period of time when they'd gone through the motions of being a family. And in the process, they'd almost become one for real. But it had taken only a carelessly spoken word, a look, to shatter that fragile structure.

"And you . . . sat . . . with me," Austin said.

It was true. She'd forgotten that, too, but now she remembered. She'd sat facing him, a lover's position.

She stood in front of him now, her hands in his. Above them, beyond the leaves, beyond the branches, beyond the jet streams, the stratosphere, and the ionosphere, was what Amy would have called a cartoon moon. Its light wasn't an intrusive light, but merely a hello. A comfort, a candle burning in the window. Beneath it, beneath the shelter of leaves, they were wrapped in the indigo velvet of the night.

He pulled her closer, so they were knee to knee. "It was . . . snowing."

Yes. It *had* been snowing. She'd forgotten that too. And now she remembered how strong his arms had been. How safe he'd made her feel with those arms around her.

Maybe she had almost loved him. Maybe she could have grown to love him, if only things had been different . . .

"I made you . . . wear . . . my coat."

He'd wrapped it around her, thick and warm and scented with the cold.

What had happened to those two people? Where had they gone?

She had no idea what made her do what she did next—she'd never initiated anything between them—but she slipped off her sandals, the grass cool and damp under her bare feet. With both hands on the ropes, she stood facing Austin, knee to knee. He gripped her waist to help steady her as she slid her legs on either side of him, her sundress riding up around her thighs.

His hands moved to her bottom, settling her more firmly against him. Then he grasped the rope, his hands just above hers.

"Ready?" he whispered.

He seemed like the old Austin. The Austin she'd forgotten but now remembered. He was strong, confident, his voice so deep it reverberated against her chest. And yet he was a different Austin too. More mature. More aware. And mixed in with those two people was a stranger, someone she didn't know at all.

Was she ready? "Yes."

And don't miss these spectacular
romances from
Bantam Books, on sale in February:

SILK AND STONE
by Deborah Smith
In the compelling tradition of *Blue Willow*,
an enchanting new novel of the heart.

LADY DANGEROUS
by the nationally bestselling author
Suzanne Robinson

SINS OF INNOCENCE
by Jean Stone
A poignant novel of four women with only
one thing in common:
each gave her baby to a stranger.

CALL JAN SPILLER'S ASTROLINE

OFFICIAL RULES

To enter the sweepstakes below carefully follow all instructions found elsewhere in this offer.

The **Winners Classic** will award prizes with the following approximate maximum values: 1 Grand Prize: $26,500 (or $25,000 cash alternate); 1 First Prize: $3,000; 5 Second Prizes: $400 each; 35 Third Prizes: $100 each; 1,000 Fourth Prizes: $7.50 each. Total maximum retail value of Winners Classic Sweepstakes is $42,500. Some presentations of this sweepstakes may contain individual entry numbers corresponding to one or more of the aforementioned prize levels. To determine the Winners, individual entry numbers will first be compared with the winning numbers preselected by computer. For winning numbers not returned, prizes will be awarded in random drawings from among all eligible entries received. Prize choices may be offered at various levels. If a winner chooses an automobile prize, all license and registration fees, taxes, destination charges and, other expenses not offered herein are the responsibility of the winner. If a winner chooses a trip, travel must be complete within one year from the time the prize is awarded. Minors must be accompanied by an adult. Travel companion(s) must also sign release of liability. Trips are subject to space and departure availability. Certain black-out dates may apply.

The following applies to the sweepstakes named above:

No purchase necessary. You can also enter the sweepstakes by sending your name and address to: P.O. Box 508, Gibbstown, N.J. 08027. Mail each entry separately. Sweepstakes begins 6/1/93. Entries must be received by 12/30/94. Not responsible for lost, late, damaged, misdirected, illegible or postage due mail. Mechanically reproduced entries are not eligible. All entries become property of the sponsor and will not be returned.

Prize Selection/Validations: Selection of winners will be conducted no later than 5:00 PM on January 28, 1995, by an independent judging organization whose decisions are final. Random drawings will be held at 1211 Avenue of the Americas, New York, N.Y. 10036. Entrants need not be present to win. Odds of winning are determined by total number of entries received. Circulation of this sweepstakes is estimated not to exceed 200 million. All prizes are guaranteed to be awarded and delivered to winners. Winners will be notified by mail and may be required to complete an affidavit of eligibility and release of liability which must be returned within 14 days of date on notification or alternate winners will be selected in a random drawing. Any prize notification letter or any prize returned to a participating sponsor, Bantam Doubleday Dell Publishing Group, Inc., its participating divisions or subsidiaries, or the independent judging organization as undeliverable will be awarded to an alternate winner. Prizes are not transferable. No substitution for prizes except as offered or as may be necessary due to unavailability, in which case a prize of equal or greater value will be awarded. Prizes will be awarded approximately 90 days after the drawing. All taxes are the sole responsibility of the winners. Entry constitutes permission (except where prohibited by law) to use winners' names, hometowns, and likenesses for publicity purposes without further or other compensation. Prizes won by minors will be awarded in the name of parent or legal guardian.

Participation: Sweepstakes open to residents of the United States and Canada, except for the province of Quebec. Sweepstakes sponsored by Bantam Doubleday Dell Publishing Group, Inc., (BDD), 1540 Broadway, New York, NY 10036. Versions of this sweepstakes with different graphics and prize choices will be offered in conjunction with various solicitations or promotions by different subsidiaries and divisions of BDD. Where applicable, winners will have their choice of any prize offered at level won. Employees of BDD, its divisions, subsidiaries, advertising agencies, independent judging organization, and their immediate family members are not eligible.

Canadian residents, in order to win, must first correctly answer a time limited arithmetical skill testing question. Void in Puerto Rico, Quebec and wherever prohibited or restricted by law. Subject to all federal, state, local and provincial laws and regulations. For a list of major prize winners (available after 1/29/95): send a self-addressed, stamped envelope entirely separate from your entry to: Sweepstakes Winners, P.O. Box 517, Gibbstown, NJ 08027. Requests must be received by 12/30/94. DO NOT SEND ANY OTHER CORRESPONDENCE TO THIS P.O. BOX.

Don't miss these fabulous Bantam women's fiction titles

on sale in February

• SILK AND STONE by Deborah Smith

From MIRACLE to BLUE WILLOW, Deborah Smith's evocative novels won a special place in reader's hearts. Now, from the author hailed by critics as "a uniquely significant voice in contemporary women's fiction," comes a spellbinding, unforgettably romantic new work. Vibrant with wit, aching with universal emotion, SILK AND STONE is Deborah Smith at her most triumphant.

_____29689-2 $5.99/$6.99 in Canada

• LADY DANGEROUS
by Suzanne Robinson

Liza Elliot had a very good reason for posing as a maid in the house of the notorious Viscount Radcliffe. It was the only way the daring beauty could discover whether this sinister nobleman had been responsible for her brother's murder. But Liza never knew how much she risked until the night she came face-to-face with the dangerously arresting and savagely handsome viscount himself.

_____29576-4 $5.50/$6.50 in Canada

• SINS OF INNOCENCE
by Jean Stone

They were four women with only one thing in common: each gave up her baby to a stranger. They'd met in a home for unwed mothers, where all they had to hold on to was each other. Now, twenty-five years later, it's time to go back and face the past.

_____56342-4 $5.99/$6.99 n Canada

**Ask for these books at your local bookstore
or use this page to order.**